CAMP Angels

CAMP Angels

JAMES L. CURRY, SR.

TATE PUBLISHING & *Enterprises*

Tate Publishing
& *Enterprises*

Tate Publishing is committed to excellence in the publishing industry. Our staff of highly trained professionals, including editors, graphic designers, and marketing personnel, work together to produce the very finest books available. The company reflects the philosophy established by the founders, based on Psalms 68:11,

"The Lord Gave The Word And Great Was The Company Of Those Who Published It."

If you would like further information, please contact us:
1.888.361.9473 | www.tatepublishing.com
Tate Publishing & *Enterprises*, LLC | 127 E. Trade Center Terrace
Mustang, Oklahoma 73064 USA

Camp Angels

This novel is a work of fiction. However, several names, descriptions, entities and incidents included in the story are based on the lives of real people.

Cover design by Jen Redden
Interior design by Chris Webb

Published in the United States of America

ISBN: 1-5988677-7-6

07.02.15

This book is dedicated to the many brave men and women that risked and lost their lives, performing courageous acts of courage while engaged in the resistance movement against Nazi Germanys Third Reich.

Acknowledgments

I would like to take this opportunity to thank all those who helped in many ways in writing this book.

Dr. Richard Tate who had confidence in my writing to go the extra mile at his own expense to see the book was written correctly.

My good friend, Larry Gunter, who proof read the book many more time than he really wanted to.

Kyle Swanson, Conceptual Editor, who edited the book and gave me very good advice and was more help than she will ever know.

My wife, Marguerite, my children who all tried to help dear old dad with my spelling and grammar.

The Los Angeles Holocaust Museum for providing such a vast amount of research materials.

1

It was the early part of December 1938, in the town of Dusseldorf, Germany. There were eight to ten inches of fresh snow and the wind was blowing across the rooftops causing the temperature to be well below zero.

The Weinstein family just finished dinner when Edward, a good-looking, mature-looking, young man, said, "But Papa, you don't understand. I am an actor! Playing the part of a German solider does not make me one. No more than buying a ticket to the symphony makes you a musician."

Mr. Weinstein was very upset with Edward, first for being an actor and second, because he failed to persuade his son to become a doctor like himself. Edward's father was a very distinguished looking gentleman and very well groomed.

"Why?" shouted Edward's father, as he pushed himself away from the table. "Why couldn't you have been like your older sisters? They both have fine professions in the medical field. Here you are, up on a stage playing make believe, as a German solider at that!"

"Leave the boy alone," cried Edward's mother, as she and Edward's two older sisters, Dorothy and Iris, cleared the table. "Let him be what he wants to be. He is making fine money being an actor."

Dorothy spoke up and said, "Papa, you have to turn loose of Edward. He is twenty-nine years old now and has to choose what he feels he can do best. It's not that he does not love you. They have made him a fine offer to go to Munich with a world-renowned production company, just turn loose of him!"

"Show your Father some respect when you speak to him," Dorothy's Mother said as she slapped the back of Dorothy's head with a cup towel.

"Mama, that hurt!" said Dorothy.

"I meant for it to hurt," she said and snickered as she rubbed the back of Dorothy's head.

Iris thought, well, everyone else has had a turn so she said, "I believe we all should be proud of Edward for his accomplishments in the theater. I know I am. And I just hope you all feel the same."

Edward got his height from his father. His two sisters got theirs from their mother. Mrs. Weinstein was short, and as they say, pleasingly plump, as were her two daughters.

Mr. Weinstein looked up and motioned to the others to gather around the chair where he was sitting. "I have something to say," he whispered, "You all know what we are going through here in Germany and you know things are only going to get worse. I have heard the Germans have started taking over the homes and businesses of the prominent Jews and moving them into the ghetto. I also hear some of the families are being taken away from the ghetto and shipped off to work camps. I don't want this to happen to us, which is one of my reasons I would prefer Edward stay close to home. I say this because if we do decide to leave Germany in a hurry, we will all be together!"

Edward shook his head side to side and said, "But Papa, that is unfair, I will only be gone for one month."

"That may be too long, Edward," Papa said, as he got up from his chair and crossed the room. Turning back in the doorway he said, "Doctor Siegel and his family have not been seen for two weeks now."

"What does that mean, Papa? How do you know they are not just off for the holidays?" asked Edward.

"I am not saying they have been picked up, Edward, I am saying maybe they have made their way out of Germany. I was talking to Isaac Rosenburg, the jeweler, yesterday and he told me the Siegel's had sold all their family jewelry.

Edward replied, "That means nothing, Papa, maybe they needed the money."

"Oh yes that's it, Edward, they needed the money to go on holiday. Why didn't I think of that? We didn't need to have this conversation at all. I don't understand you, Edward. Are you blind to what is going on?" said Papa.

"I understand, Papa; the Jews in Poland are having a time of it. But that does not mean we Jews here in Germany are going to have any problems," Edward said.

"It's happening here as well, Edward. I just want you to take these facts into consideration before you make your decision to take off and play in your dream world. In fact, I would rather you join the resistance movement and fight the Germans rather than entertain them! I am going to bed now," replied Papa.

As Edward's mother turned to follow Papa out of the room, she stopped, looked at Edward, and said, "Do what you feel is best for you, Edward; everything will be all right. Good night, children."

Against his father's wishes, Edward decided to go to Munich. Edward's mother and sisters were at the train station to see him off. The train to Munich was to leave at 8:15 p.m.

"Go back home now, mama, it's too cold for you to be out. I'll be all right," Edward said, checking his watch. "Only fifteen more minutes."

Mama pulled Edward's cap off, brushed his hair out of his eyes, and said, "Papa said to tell you he couldn't get away to see you off."

"I understand, Mama. I am glad you and the girls made it. But I wish you would go home now. Really, I'll be all right," said Edward.

Mama asked Edward, "Will we get to meet this person that thinks so much of you that he wants to take you off to Munich?"

"He hardly even knows me, Mama, we have only met one time and that was for less than an hour. I was recommended to him. And no, you will not get to meet him, as he gets on the train at the station before this one," answered Edward.

Edward stepped up onto the train when he heard the train whistle make a shrill noise and saw the train start to move. Edward's mother and sisters took a few steps forward and were waving their handkerchiefs and bidding him a farewell, when both Dorothy and Iris yelled at the same time, "Good luck, Edward!"

"Thank you!" Edward yelled back, "Tell Papa I understand. And tell him Munich is not that far from Dusseldorf. It's not like I am going out of the country. See you in a month."

There was a chill in Edward's compartment to the point he was uncomfortable and was unable to enjoy the view of the countryside. Even though it was dark outside, with the full moon reflecting off the bright snow, it didn't seem to hamper his view. Still, he wanted to be comfortable, so he called for the car attendant and asked if there was something he could do to warm up the compartment.

The attendant, a big red-faced German with the voice of a whisky tenor, said he would try. As he was closing the door, Edward heard him mumble under his breath, "These finicky Jews are never satisfied."

Edward wondered, why would he say that? Everyone is always mistaking him for a German. He spoke German fluently. He glanced over, spotted his brown leather case on the seat next to him and saw his mother had put a large white tag with his name printed in red, "Edward Weinstein," as if he were going off to school or something.

Edward remembered what his father had said about the Siegel family not being seen for over two weeks, and thought that maybe his father might have been overreacting. Maybe the doctor had a holiday planned and just failed to mention it to anyone. The whole family skied and it was an ideal time to head for the mountains. There was no answer for why they sold their family jewelry.

Edward looked at his watch and remembered the director, Mr. Felmen, had invited him to meet some of the other cast members in the club car.

There were about twelve to thirteen members already there when Edward entered the car. He could hear Mr. Felmen as he went over some details of the play. Not wanting to disturb him, he slipped into the first chair he came to. As he slithered into the chair, he had not noticed the small table with an empty wine bottle and two wineglasses sitting on it, which he hit straight on with his elbow, causing everyone in the car to look in his direction.

Mr. Felmen, taking advantage of Edward's tardiness and interruption, said in a very loud voice, "Oh, I see Mr. Weinstein has arrived! I believe you are playing a medical officer in this play, am I correct? Or is it a drunken soldier?"

The car roared with laughter. Edward was too embarrassed for words. He tried to apologize, but the more he said, the worse it got.

Mr. Felmen said, "I hope you don't muddle your lines in the play as you are doing now, Mr. Weinstein."

"No, sir. I'll do better," said Edward. While Edward was having this conversation with Mr. Felmen, he couldn't help but notice a very pretty young lady with short brown hair and smiling eyes looking at him very attentively. Not wanting to miss the chance of meeting her, he excused himself and again apologized to Mr. Felmen for the disturbance.

Edward made his way across the car and introduced himself to the young lady, "Hello, I am Edward Weinstein. Are you one of the cast members?"

"No, I am not. My name is Sylvia and I attend The University of Munich. I am taking a holiday with my father."

"What a coincidence, both of my sisters attended there. What is your major?" Edward asked.

"Medicine," she answered, as she twisted the empty wineglass between her index finger and her thumb.

Edward said, "My sisters also majored in medicine," and added, "Can I get us a couple of drinks?"

"Yes, thank you," she replied and then asked, "What are their names?"

"What, the drinks or my sisters?" Edward asked.

"Your two sisters, silly!" And then added, "I'll have a glass of white wine, thank you."

"Okay, I'll get the drinks and then tell you about my dear sisters. Why don't you grab those two chairs behind you. I'll be right back," said Edward.

Handing Sylvia her drink and setting his on the table between them, he said, "Now about my two sisters. Dorothy is the eldest at 34 and then there is Iris; she is 31. I believe you are a little too young to have known them, as they both attended the university some time ago."

"That is true, but maybe they would remember my father, or if they took drama classes, my father may remember them. He was the drama coach there for twelve years or so," she said looking up over her wineglass as she took a sip.

"You say you are traveling with your Father? I would like to meet him and ask him if he may have known my sisters," said Edward.

Sylvia started to choke. Grabbing a napkin off the table and wiping off her chin, she started to laugh.

"Are you all right?" he asked, handing her additional napkins.

"Yes, thank you. You have met my Father," replied Sylvia.

"I have?" asked Edward.

"Yes." She could hardly control her laughter. "He is the director, Mr. Felmen."

Edward looked in the direction of Mr. Felmen, and even though he was having a conversation with a couple of young cast members, his eyes were boring down on Edward. "My, oh my, but it is a small world." They both began to laugh. Edward stood and reaching for Sylvia's glass, he asked, "Can I get you another?"

Before she could answer a voice from over Edward shoulder said, "Yes, why don't you get me another drink also Mr. Weinstein or do you prefer to be called Edward?" Mr. Felmen asked.

"Edward is fine, sir. What are you drinking, sir?" replied Edward.

"I'll have a Gin and Tonic with a lime twist, please." Edward heading back with the drinks noticed Sylvia and her father had moved to a couch and chair arrangement. Mr. Felmen was sitting in the chair.

"Here we are, a white wine for the lady a Gin and Tonic with a lime twist for the gentleman." Edward held his glass at eye level and said, "Cheers."

After clicking their glasses together, Mr. Felmen, a heavy-set man with a graying beard and thick horn rimmed glasses pulled himself forward in the chair and in a low voice said, "Edward, there are a couple of things I would like to talk to you about. I am not sure you are aware of our situation. I don't know how long we are going to be able to continue to produce the play before the Germans discover that eighty percent of the players are Jewish. It has not been a problem in the past, but now it is different."

Edward interrupted by asking. "Are you aware of any Jewish families here in Germany loosing their homes and/or having their business's taken away by the German Police?"

Mr. Felmen looked concerned and said, "I think we should go back to my compartment to finish this conversation. For your information Edward, if you come alone, I am in drawing room twelve, two cars back."

Sylvia said, "I'll come along also, father."

"Well then, you two finish your drinks and stroll back in, let's say in a half hour, okay?" said Felmen.

Sylvia could see the concerned look on Edward's face. They both started to speak at the same time when Edward said. "Excuse me, go ahead."

Sylvia continued, "I hope Father did not make you uneasy with his concerns."

"No, that's not it. They are the same concerns my father has and the biggest reason for him not wanting me to go on this trip," replied Edward.

A couple of young men approached Edward and Sylvia and introduced themselves as cast members. The one introducing himself as Otto looked as if he could have been a body builder, and the other one calling himself Fritz looked as if he had been sick for a while. Both men had their hair short, like a military cut. Otto asked Sylvia if Mr. Felmen was her Father.

"Yes, he is," she replied. "Have you worked under his direction before?"

"No, we have not. We are like Mr. Weinstein here, we were all brought over from the Mueller productions after the play "An Alternative" closed and have been offered parts in your Fathers production," said Otto.

"Oh it's not his production, he is only directing it," said Sylvia.

"Didn't he also write it?" asked Otto.

"Yes he did. But what I meant is he is not the producer," Sylvia replied.

Otto asked, "Is he the same Felmen that was at the University of Munich?"

"Yes, he is," Sylvia answered. "What parts do you two portray in the play?" She asked.

"Oh well, we are only medics for part of the play and then we are wounded soldiers toward the end," he replied.

"Are you two in any of my scenes?" Edward asked.

Otto looking at his friend Fritz, replied, "I don't believe so."

Edward, checking his watch said, "Well, I hate to be a party pooper but Mr. Felmen asked me to stop by his compartment before I turn in." He stands, taking Sylvia's hand and asked, "Shall we go?"

"Yes," she replied, knowing Edward was making up the part of her father wanting to go over his lines, but she felt uneasy answering their questions and felt it was time to leave.

Otto asked, "What hotel are you staying in?"

Edward answered, "Hotel Regent."

"Is that near the theater?' Otto asked.

"No, it is next to the train station at city center," Edward said, as he turned and walked away.

Otto said, "Fine, if we don't see you again before the train arrives, we will see you at the theater."

ב

The train caused Sylvia and Edward to sway from left to right as they hurried along the aisle.

Sylvia looking back over her shoulder, whispered to Edward, “I wonder what that was all about? Don’t you think they were a bit forward, asking questions about my Father like that?”

“Yes I do,” Edward answered knocking on Mr. Felmen’s compartment door. The door swung open, Mr. Felmen ushered the two inside, and leaned out into the aisle taking a quick look to his left and right before closing and latching the door.

Before Sylvia’s Father could say, sit down; Sylvia started telling him about the two young men.

“Well, what did they say?” He asked.

“First off, they wanted to know if you were my father and then asked if you were the same Felmen who worked at the University of Munich,” Sylvia replied.

“Were they German?” He asked as he poured a glass of wine and motioned to ask if they would care for one also.

“I assume they were, with names like Otto and Fritz,” she replied.

Edward spoke up and said, “Otto told us they were both brought over from the Mueller productions as I had been!”

“That is incorrect,” Felmen said, as he gulped down his glass of wine. “You were the only one hired from that production. Did you recognize them? What were their ages?”

“No, I can’t say I recognized them but then there were a lot of cast members in that play, and as for their ages, I would say they were my age twenty-nine or so.” He held out their wineglasses for Mr. Felmen to fill. Edward had seen this concerned expression on Mr. Felmen’s face earlier in the club car.

Sylvia seeing the expression on her father’s face asked, “What do you think this is all about Dad?” As she reached out and placed her hand on his forearm.

Her father placed his hand on hers and said, “I am not sure just now but as I discussed in the club car. I am afraid times are changing at such a rapid pace,” Felmen, in a low voice, said, “Earlier Edward, you asked me if I had heard of any Jewish families in Germany being taken away by the German Police. My answer is no, not here in Germany, but my mother and younger sister and her family are living in Copenhagen, where they do not distinguish between Jews and non-Jews. There were rumors of a German military build-up, but late last year my mother told me she had heard Hitler promised not to invade Denmark, which made her and my sister and family feel relatively safe. But now with the German build-up, the Gestapo has set up a ghetto, concentrating all of the Jews there. It is just a matter of time before they are rounded up with the others. I am working with some friends to get them, along with Sylvia, into Switzerland, before they are sent to the ghetto and then taken to a work camp. The Germans are looking for me now, and if they catch me, they will charge me with Political Subversive activity, as well as belonging to the resistance movement. I joined the resistance as a courier but I have become more involved. Recently when the Gestapo began hunting down Danish Jews I began to help these families flee the Country. And of course, all my plays are of a seditious nature to the Third Reich. And that my friend, is why I am no longer with the University of Munich!" Felmen poured himself another drink and leaned back against the big seat cushion and said, "I am not getting off this train, and have a couple of snivel nose German boys turn me in to the Gestapo."

Sylvia looked at Edward and said, "Dad has had too much to drink. We have to stay on the train with him. I know you didn't know anything about this, but Father and I have tickets for Obereberfing just below Lake Starnberger; it is a small town about twenty-five miles south of Munich. We had no intentions of staying in Munich. There is an hour layover there, we are going to get off the train, giving everyone time to leave the station, before re-boarding and continuing on to Oberebering. They will not be looking for you, so you could get off, purchase a ticket for Obereberfing, and go with us. We can't let him get off the train and hang around for an hour, he will be caught," she whispered.

Edward thought about what his father had said about joining the resistance and he was right. He asked Sylvia, "Do you think maybe your father's friends could help me get my parents and sisters out of Germany?"

"I don't know, we will ask him when he wakes up," she said, as she covered her Father with his overcoat.

Edward got up, and unlatching the door, turned and said, "When we get into Munich, this will be the first place they will look if they do not see your Father get off the train, so you will have to move into my compartment number twenty-three one-car back. No one will look for you there. We will figure something out. Let him sleep it off for an hour or so. I am going back to the club car and check something out."

Edward made his way back to the club car just as the train stopped in Nuremberg. He did not see Otto and his friend Fritz in the club car. But as he turned to go back to Mr. Felmen's compartment he glanced to the far end of the club car and noticed that Otto and Fritz were leaving the train. He went into the next car; it was a sleeper, so he opened the door to the men's wash room, and saw no one was there. He switched off the light prior to entering so not to be seen from the outside. He saw the two young men standing on the platform talking to a German Officer just below the window he was looking out. He was startled at first, but realized even if he had left the lights on, no one could see into the window because it was a one way glass, viewable only from the inside out. He could not hear what they were saying to the German Officer, but Edward caught a glimpse of a photo of Mr. Felmen as the officer was folding up some official looking documents and placing them into a briefcase. The officer handed the case to a young soldier, and motioned for him to leave. The young soldier snapped to attention and saluted the officer before turning to leave. Edward heard the shrill whistle and knew the two would be returning to the train. He got to his feet, made his way out of the men's wash room, and darted between the sleeper and the club car before they had a chance to see him.

Edward knocked on Felmen's compartment door and said, "It's me Edward, open up." The door opened and Edward saw Sylvia walking back over and placing a damp wash clothe on her Father's forehead.

Edward switched off the light and took a quick look out the window to see if he could spot the German Officer. "There he is! Do you recognize that German Officer standing there by the baggage cart?" He asked Felmen.

Felmen rose up and removed the washcloth from his forehead and glanced outside just in time to see him and said, "Yes, that is

Oscar Ludwig. He is the same man responsible for my dismissal from the University, but he was not wearing a uniform then!"

"Well, our two young German friends from the club car, were talking to him and he was showing them your photo. I am sure they will be in Munich waiting for you. I suggest you shave off your beard and have Sylvia cut your hair," Edward said, pulling down the compartment shades.

Felmen apologized to Edward and his daughter for having too much to drink and added, "I am okay now, and have my wits about me."

There was a knock at the door and Felmen put his finger to his lips and waved his other hand quickly from left to right. "Who is it?"

A voice came from the other side of the door. "The attendant. Do you wish for your bed to be turned down now, Sir?"

Felmen in a loud voice answered, "No, thank you. I will call for you later."

"Yes, Sir," the attendant said. Felmen listened for a moment and could hear the attendant knocking on the compartment next door.

"We must get off the train before Munich. We can get off at the next station, which is Ingolstadt. We will be able to get a car and drive onto Obereberfing. It will be safer that way," he said as he took the scissors and started clipping away at his beard. He asked Edward if he had a shaving mug and brush.

Edward said, "Yes, I will go get it." Edward returned and set the mug next to the washbasin where Felmen was clipping away at his beard. Before long Felmen was ready to lather up and soon after his face was clean-shaven.

Sylvia said, "Sit here Dad, and I'll trim your hair." She started snipping the scissors and slapping them against the comb she was holding.

When she was finished Edward said, "There is no way anyone would recognize you now. I think we should clean up the evidence of your shaving and haircut or they will know you have changed your identity." Edward placed all the clippings into the toilet and held the handle down making sure all the evidence was flushed down the drain.

"Mr. Felmen? I ask asked Sylvia while you were napping if there was a possibility your friends could help me get my parents and sisters out of Germany, and into Switzerland?" said Edward.

"I am not sure Edward, but I'll do everything possible to help you. I feel I owe you that much. I was wrong in asking you to go to Munich to work in the play, knowing I had no intention of even starting it, but as I said earlier I have gotten deeply involved with the resistance movement and was asked to hire you for the play. I told the contact to see you at the theater. They know I had no intention of going there, but I knew you would," replied Felmen.

Sylvia said, "I have to agree with my Father. We are both sorry we got you mixed up in this."

Edward thinking again of what his Father said, told them both, "It is not your fault. My ego got the best of me and now I am more concerned about my parents and sisters safety than I am about my career as an actor."

"Well," Felmen said, "If it is any consolation, you did come with a high recommendation."

Edward wanted to say it's not! But instead said thank you.

Felmen said to Sylvia, "We should start gathering our things together, we are getting close to Ingolstadt."

Edward said, as he turned to leave, "I do not believe our friends are going to make contact with anyone else tonight but to be sure, I'll go forward and check them out. I'll be back before it is time for us to get off."

Felmen said, "You don't have to get off with us Edward. Sylvia and I have false papers that authorize us to travel to Obereberfing, your papers are only good for Munich. My friends will still be contacting you at the theater."

"I believe the less our German friends see of me the better. They could make it very uncomfortable for my family and me with their questions about your whereabouts," said Edward.

Mr. Felmen said, "I would have to agree with you," as Edward shut the door.

Edward made his way forward again. He did not see the two young men in the club car, in fact there was no one there, but the car attendant and it looked as if he was getting ready to close up the car for the night. Sylvia and her Father were all ready to go when Edward knocked on the door. As he steps inside, he said, "There was no sign of Otto or Fritz."

3

They went back to Edward's compartment so he could gather his things. As they stepped down from the train they starting walking toward the rear, instead of toward the station. They hoped the other passengers would think they were boarding the train.

After walking toward the end of the train for a while Felmen said, "Let's wait here until the train pulls out, just in case they also got off."

They waited until after the train pulled out of the station. Evidently the two young Germans were fast asleep in their cozy sleeper car. As they entered the station Felmen said, "Let's leave our bags here by the door. Edward, you and Sylvia go pick us up some sandwiches and coffee. Sylvia knows how I like it. I'll make a call to my friends and have them bring a car to the station. The sooner we are on our way the better." Reaching into his pocket Felman brings out some loose change for the phone call. After speaking with his friends and hanging up the receiver, he felt a tap on his shoulder. As he turned to see who it was, he hoped the German officer tapping on his shoulder did not suspect anything from his shocked expression.

"Do you have change for ten Marks?" He asked.

"Yes, I believe I do," Felmen said as he started counting out the change into the Officer's hand. He turned quickly and started to walk away.

"Hey!" The officer yelled. Felmen turned back around and the Officer held out his hand saying, "Here are your ten marks."

Felmen felt as if his knees were going to buckle. The officer asked, "Are you all right?"

"Yes, but I am a bit hungry. My daughter and her husband are over picking up something for me right now. Thank you." Felmen figured if they were looking for him they would be looking for a man traveling alone with his daughter, not someone traveling with a daughter and a son in-law.

Sylvia saw the Officer talking to her Father just at the time he held out his hand and handed her father something. She was too far away to distinguish what it was. She nudged Edward and nodded toward her Father and said, "Let's wait here to see what happens." They saw her Father turn and walk away.

He noticed them standing by the food vendor cart and approached them saying, "I am not very good at this kind of stuff. Maybe they had justification for dismissing me as the drama coach. I can't act! I talked to my good friend, Preben. His people are delivering a car to us, so let's go stand outside the station."

"What did that German officer hand you?" Sylvia asked as she was handing him a sandwich and a cup of coffee.

"I had given him change for ten marks and was in such a hurry to get away from him that I forgot to take his ten marks. By the way Edward, I told Preben to call ahead to Obereberfing and have papers made up for you as well. Preben told me that Julius would make arrangements to have our wardrobe trunks picked up from the theater. He said we would have need of them."

"Aren't you worried about what the other cast members; let

alone the producer will say? Won't they be suspicious and wonder what happened to us?" Edward asked.

"Not now. They knew I wasn't showing up and I told Preben you would be with us. No one knows about you being brought over from the Mueller Production other than our contacts," Felman said.

Sylvia interrupted asking, "How about the two Germans, Otto and Fritz. They said they had been brought over from the Mueller Productions like Edward had."

"That was just their story," Felmen said and continued, "They were most likely following me in the first place and knew that I had asked the cast members to meet in the club car for a little get together and drinks."

"How would they know about the get together?" Edward asked, taking a big bite out of his sandwich.

Felmen said, "I believe I know who it is and she is still on the train. Most likely she was told to stay out of site after our two new friends made contact. She knows nothing else about what my plans are. I bet the German Officer on the platform talking to Otto and Fritz convinced her to cooperate with the German police and pass on any information she might have about my whereabouts and activities. She is not a threat. She is just a young German girl from the theater trying to get ahead in life." They saw the flicker of the headlights of an on coming car pulling into the front of the station with a second car close behind.

Felmen instructed Edward and Sylvia to put the bags into the front car. "I'll be right back," he said. He approached the second car, bent down, and greeted the person sitting in the passenger's seat by shaking his hand, opening the door, and stepping back so they could get out.

"It's been a long time Preben!" Felmen said as they walked over toward the building. Preben turned and walked back over to the car, opened the door, and reached in for the lighter and stuck it to the cigarette he held in his mouth. Preben was tall and slender and very handsome. He had a nervous habit of rubbing his chin. He walked over to where Felmen was standing. The person driving the first car finished helping put the bags into the car and joined them. There was the sound of a loud whistle coming from the front door of the building They looked and saw a large German Police Officer walking toward them waving his hands and pointing up to a sign with big red letters and yelling, "Rauchen Verboten, kannst du nicht sehen?" (No Smoking, are you blind?)

Felmen, knowing Preben did not speak German, said under his breath, "Put your cigarette out, there is no smoking here!"

"I am sorry," Preben said, taking the cigarette out of his mouth and stomping it out on the ground. He turned, walked to the car, and waved to Felmen. The other person that was standing with Felmen joined Preben and got into the driver's seat and they sped away.

The Policeman turned and walked back into the station. Felmen got in the car on the driver's side and drove out of the station.

"There should be a map in the glove box, let's take a look to see where we are going," Felmen said, as he pulled over to study the map. "Obereberfing is twenty-five miles due south from Munich. We are at least an hour or so from Munich. The train is a half-hour ahead of us; therefore it should be there at 6:30 a.m. We are going to go around Munich approximately fifty miles out of our way, but I am not taking any chances they may figure out what we have done and set up roadblocks." Edward was sitting up front with Felmen while Sylvia was stretched out across the back seat using her father's overcoat to cover herself. Both were fast asleep until Felmen turned the car quickly and hit a few ruts driving up in front of a hotel.

"What is wrong?" Sylvia cried.

"Sorry about that dear. I am going to pick up some coffee. You two want a cup?" Felman asked.

They both said, "Yes, that would be fine."

Edward added, "Do you want me to drive now?"

"Okay with me," Felmen said.

It was a small hotel and the kitchen was closed at that hour but the clerk said, "We have coffee for the staff, would you like a cup?" Felmen felt embarrassed having to ask for three cups. The clerk said, "No problem, we have plenty. Complements of the hotel."

As Felmen turned to leave, he slipped five marks under the pad on the counter and said in German, "Danke schüen." (Thank you very much).

Getting into the car, he handed them their coffee and said, "Sorry there are no rolls. The kitchen wasn't open for breakfast yet, we were lucky to get the coffee."

"How much farther Dad?" Sylvia asked.

"Oh, I would say another hour or so. Going around the long way has taken us longer than I thought," said Felman.

Edward adjusted the driver's seat and pulled out into the morning traffic. Later that morning, Edward saw the sign for Obereberfing, 5 kilometers. He pulled over and woke Felmen up by nudging him and said, "We are just pulling into Obereberfing. Where do we go from here?"

Felmen pointed and said, "Pull up to that phone booth just ahead. I have to makc a couple of calls." Felmen made his calls, returned to the car, and said, "There will be another car here in a few minutes."

They didn't have to wait long until they saw a car pull up behind them and two men got out and walked up to the passengers window. One of the men motioned for Felmen to roll the window down and leaned in and asked Edward for the car keys.

He took them and handed the keys to the other man standing with him and instructed him to open the trunk.

The man opened the trunk and asked, "Does everything go?"

Edward got out, walked to the rear of the car, and answered, "Yes!" as he started taking out the bags and handing them to the man.

Felmen told his daughter and Edward to get into the other car. He then got back into the car he had been riding in. The man, who earlier had asked Edwards for the keys, got in holding a brief case and said to Felman, "I hardly recognized you without your beard."

"Yes, I had to remove it and cut my hair so not to be recognized when I got off the train. Edward saw a photo of me that Ludwig was showing two young Germans who were asking a lot of question on the train. That is why we got off before Munich, or I am sure I would have been arrested," Felmen said extending his hand toward Julius to shake his hand.

Julius, in his early forties, was like Edward's father. He was a very distinguished looking man; heavy-set but by no means fat. He was solid as a rock. You could see his daily work out and jogging had paid off.

"Do you have all the papers in order?" asked Felmen.

Julius answered, "Yes," and handed the case on his lap to Felmen. "All the necessary papers for the upcoming operation are in the case and these are for Edward to use just in case you get stopped. Here is the address and directions. The phone is safe for you to use. The wardrobe trunks will arrive in a couple of days. I do have very bad news Melvin," as he called Felmen by his first name. "Your Mother and Sister have been picked up and moved into the ghetto. They did not get your brother in-law or the two children. We are working on getting them into Switzerland. It could be a matter of days before your mother and sister are assigned to a work camp. We have issued orders supposedly for them to be taken to a work camp and are sending a couple of our men to escort them out of the ghetto and into Switzerland. We have to work fast; therefore you will not have a chance to see them before they leave. You are not to try to contact them in any way. As I told you, we have plans for your young man Edward. We will be contacting him in a few days. Our plans also include your daughter as well, so her departure to Switzerland will have to be delayed."

Felmen felt sick and asked, "Am I included in your plans?"

"No! You are too close to the situation and the Gestapo knows you. Weinstein and your daughter are not known," said Julius.

"They are now," said Felmen. "Those two young Germans on the train asked my daughter questions about me. They also met Edward and knew we had brought him over from the Mueller productions."

"That won't matter. Where Edward and Sylvia are going to be assigned, no one will know them," Julius said as he shook Felmen's hand. "Again Melvin, everything is going to work out with your mother and sister."

"What if Edward or my daughter don't want to get involved with your plans?" Felmen asked.

"We are assuming a lot, but I believe they will. You are not to discuss this with either of them. Is that understood?" Julius asked.

"Yes, but I had to tell Edward something. He knew we were not going on into Munich. I don't know what you have planned for him and I told him that already. I told him someone would be contacting him at the theater, but that has all changed now. Also, I will have to tell my daughter about her Grandmother and Aunt," he said.

Julius replied, "Yes, I understand."

Felmen shook his hand again and got out of the car. As Felmen got into the car where Sylvia and Edward were waiting, he handed Edward the envelope with his papers and said, "Look these over and memorize the information." He also handed him the directions and said, "Okay, where do we go from here?"

Following the direction Edward read to him, they pulled into a long driveway. The house was secluded, up in the woods and was completely furnished with everything necessary for ten people to live there for a month or so.

4

Meanwhile, at the Munich train station, the Gestapo had ordered the German Police to search the train. They assumed Felmen had gotten off between Nuremberg and Munich. "The train made three stops between there and here!" the Gestapo Officer said as he slapped the palm of his hand with his gloves.

"I know Felmen was on the train after we left Nuremberg," Otto said. "When we left the station I wanted to verify he was still on the train, so I had the attendant check to see if Felmen wanted the bed turned down. The attendant, after checking all the compartments in that car, told me Felmen was still in his compartment and had advised him he would call him later. I checked with the attendant just a few minutes ago and he said, "Felmen never contacted him."

"Do you think he is headed for Copenhagen to see if he can help his Mother?" asked Fritz.

The Gestapo Officer asking all the question of Otto and Fritz said, "That would be a futile attempt. Berlin has issued orders for his Mother and sister to be taken out of the Ghetto and placed in a work camp. They're sending an escort to pick them up. His brother-in-law and his two children have not been located, as of yet. But we will get them all, in due time."

"What about his daughter and the young man, Weinstein?" asked Otto.

The Officer said, as he puts his legs up on the desk and leaned back in the swivel chair, "Oh, I am sure they got off the train with him. But he is very smart and would have them go to the theater and act as if nothing had happened. Were they both in the play?"

"No, I don't believe so. Only Weinstein was in the play," Fritz said.

"Well, we will watch the theater and when he shows up we will have him in for questioning. She may well stay with her father," said the Officer.

Otto said, "I have checked at the Hotel Regent next door where Weinstein has reservation, but he hasn't checked in yet."

Meanwhile, Edward tried and was unable to contact his family on the safe phone.

"Maybe they have just stepped out for a while," said Felmen, trying to assure Edward that everything was fine.

Three days had passed from the time of their arrival to when, as they had been told, the wardrobe trunks arrived. That was a very large moving van, Felmen thought for just a couple of wardrobe trunks. To his surprise there was one additional item they did not expect. It was the ambulance they were going to use in the play.

Felmen asked the driver, a young man of nineteen or twenty, with teeth as white as snow,. "How did you swing getting this?" as he touched the fender of the vehicle.

"Oh, we have our ways," explained the driver, and added, "Julius will be here in the morning to discuss the operation plans with you." As he closed the big doors on the moving van, he asked one of the other men that came with him, "Did you park the ambulance in the shed out behind the house?"

"Yes," he said and jumped up in the front seat.

As the driver got into the truck and shut the door he leaned his head out the window and yelled, over the noise of the engine, "Julius said he would be bringing a female with him. She is part of the plan and will be working with Weinstein and your daughter."

Sylvia and Edward were down by a small frozen creek that ran through the property. Sylvia was telling Edward about her Grandmother and Aunt, "Father told me a man named Julius and his people were working on getting them into Switzerland."

Felmen joined them and told them about the wardrobe trunks and the ambulance arriving.

Sylvia asked, "What ambulance?"

"It's the ambulance from the play. They parked it in the shed out behind the house," Felmen replied.

"What do we need that for?" asked Edward.

Felmen answered, "I am not sure yet, but my friend Julius will explain in the morning. The driver of the truck said Julius would be bringing a female out with him tomorrow morning to go over the operation plan with us."

Edward told Felmen how sorry he was to hear about his mother and sister, and he hoped everything would work out for them.

Felmen said, "Thank you. Julius is working on getting them out of the country."

"Yes, Sylvia told me," said Edward.

Sylvia made dinner, but no one seemed to be very hungry. They all retired to the study where Edward made a fire. Felmen filled their glasses with wine. They all seemed to settle into their own thoughts. Edward placed a second call to his parents, still no answer!

To appease Edward, Felmen said, "I will ask Julius in the morning if maybe he could get some information on your parents."

Felmen opened another bottle of wine and filled everyone's glasses and said, "It is sad to think of what is happening in this world today. Have we all gone mad?"

Sylvia crossed the room and sat on the floor next to her Father's chair and said, "I am so glad Mother is not here to experience the horrible time we are going through." Sylvia thought and remembered she had only seen her Father cry once before and that was when her Mother passed away.

Edward threw another log on the fire and thought of how very blessed he was to have both of his parents.

Felmen put his hand on his daughter's head and started caressing her hair. Sylvia started to cry and said, "Dad, I know you are suffering now because of all the memories of Mother, as well as your concern for Grandmother and Aunt Gloria, but everything will be all right. Your friend Julius seems to be doing everything he can do and Grandmother knows you will do what you can to help them. They don't expect anything more."

Early the next morning, Felmen returned from a brisk walk to see Julius and the others going into the house. Taking only the time to stomp the snow from his boots, he was in the door before they had time to take off their coats and make formal introductions.

"Everyone, this is my daughter Sylvia and our good friend, Edward Weinstein," said Felmen.

Julius shook their hands and said, "Pleased to meet you both." He turned, stepped aside, and introduced Ethel, an attractive young lady with short brown hair who was around the same age as Sylvia. "This is the young lady I spoke to you about working with Sylvia and Edward."

Sylvia and Edward glanced at each other with blank looks.

Julius continued to introduce the others in the group, "And

this," placing his hands on the tallest of the two men's shoulder, "Is Louis." Louis was a good looking, well-groomed man in his thirties. "He will be taking your photographs for your identification cards and other documentation requiring a photo." He turned, placing his hand on the shorter of the two young men, and said says, "You have met Aurek Meirtchak, our moving van driver."

"Let's go into the study where it is warm. Maybe Ethel could help Sylvia with the coffee," Felmen suggested as he ushered them into the study.

After some small talk and a second pot of coffee, Julius stood and walked over in front of the fireplace. Next to him was an artist easel Aurek had set-up and placed charts on earlier.

Julius said, "Louis you can be excused. I will be sending down each person requiring a photo throughout the day. Everything is set up in the basement, I believe you know where things are, right?"

Louis gathered up his equipment setting next to his chair and said, "Yes, thank you."

"Friends, I ask you to hold all your questions until the briefing is completed. We hope to complete this briefing in a couple of days. First off, Edward, let me explain where you fit into the picture. We have had our eyes on you for some time now. Our contact in Dusseldorf, set it up with Felmen to offer you a part in the play he recently wrote and was going to direct. We asked Felmen not to discuss any of this with you. For one reason, Felmen doesn't really know the plan himself, only parts of it. I understand he had to tell you of our interest, but that is all he knew to tell you. This is our plan. I will start by saying you are not obligated, in any way, to join the movement and take on this assignment. Like I told Felmen, we are assuming a lot in even asking you, but we do ask you to hear us out and then decide if you think you can, or can not handle this assignment. Of course this goes for you too, Sylvia," said Julius.

Julius started flipping over the pages of charts until he came to one showing an organizational chart and explained, "We have one doctor, two nurses, and one medical assistant. This is no reflection on you, Aurek, but Edward will play the Doctor, and of course Sylvia and Ethel will play the nurses, leaving you to be the medical assistant, as well as the ambulance driver. There should be no problem with the language, as each of you speak, read, and write German fluently. Edward you will have signed orders from Joseph Mengele and counter signed by SS-Reichsfuehrer Heinrich Himmler to perform tests and research on prisoners at Mauthausen Concentration Camp. Mauthausen is a Class III Camp where prisoners and their families classified as "Return undesired" are sent. It is a punishment camp where the inmates have to do hard time in a rock quarry. Those on the punishment detail have to carry granite boulders up the 186 steps, of what they call the "stairs of death," on their backs. You and your staff will have free reign of the camp. The prisoners picked for testing will be of your choosing. We have all the pertinent documentation made up for each of you. We only have to add your photographs."

Julius took a sip of his coffee and continued by asking Felmen, "Do you have the case with the envelopes I gave you the other night?"

"Yes," Felmen said as he left the room momentarily. Returning, he walked over and handed the case containing the envelopes to Julius.

Julius opened the case, handed the envelopes to Felmen, and instructed him to pass them out adding, "You will see their real name on each envelope. Please, let's work with one individual at a time. We will start with Captain Kurt Von Mueller, Medical Doctor. We haven't much time before we put our plan into action.

Therefore, it is imperative that each one of you study and commit to memory every minute detail of the person you will be impersonating. Edward, you will have Sylvia and Ethel to help you with the medical terms and they will administer all shots. Your performance in the play "An Alternative" gives you the basic knowledge to play the part of the doctor. However, I can not express enough, the importance of knowing every detail of your character. Where did he go to school? When did he graduate? How many siblings' does he have? Are his parents alive? This goes for each one of you! You have to be comfortable being that person. Edward, it will be your responsibility to convince the camp commandant SS-Haupturmfuehrer Lukas Wiesbaden and his Deputy Gorge Bachmann that the testing and research you are performing is a vital part of the Third Reich's war effort, and has the full support of both Doctor Joseph Mengele and Heinrich Himmler. As far as the Commandant and his Deputy knows, you will be conducting tests and experiments using a brain deterioration drug. The prisoners will be given an injection that will put them into a stupor so as to appear their brain is starting to decay. These injections are not dangerous and have no lingering effects. You are not to inform the prisoners that the tests are not real. The risk is too high. If anyone in that camp found out what you are really doing, you would last about ten minutes and the operation would be a total failure. I wish we could get more out, but we are limited to six prisoners per month. You will be removing these prisoners every thirty days and transporting them to Stuttgart, supposedly for medical demonstrations and evaluation along with camp doctors from other concentration camps. Instead, you will deliver the prisoners to a designated location, for shipment to Switzerland. There is such a program at present; each camp provides six prisoners once a month, but not all camps are involved. We have an agent working within the German Army. He is responsible for assigning the camps that will take part in such experiments. Camp Mauthausen will never be assigned to perform this program; therefore there will never be an investigation or audits conducted at Camp Mauthausen, and you will not be responsible for the accountability of the prisoners. However, you will be required to maintain false documentation just in case the Camp Commandant or any of his staff gets nosey. Aurek you will be responsible for this task. Your drive from Mauthausen to Stuttgart is approximately three hundred and twenty-five miles and should take you around six to seven hours."

Julius checked his watch and said, "Let's break for lunch now. I ask you to refrain from discussing this matter until we resume the orientation after lunch. I have brought prepared sandwiches for today, and I will ask the young ladies if maybe they could prepare sandwiches for tomorrow's lunch, after they prepare tonight's dinner. The gentlemen will be packing up the ambulance with medical supplies, along with additional uniforms and equipment. I might add that I will be preparing breakfast in the morning. Don't worry, there are trained nurses on staff!"

They all chuckled and moved into the dinning room where Sylvia and Ethel started passing out Braunschweiger on rye, a hefty serving of Bavarian winekraut, and fresh coffee. There was a large bowl setting in the center of the table with mustard and onions.

Throughout the remaining part of the day, Julius continued to work with each individual and sent them down for photos. Each one having their photo taken had to put on their uniform from the waist up. Louis explained to each person that they will be required to sign over the photo, as well as on the documents themselves.

Julius closed the briefing by saying, "We have come a long way for the first day and may be able to wrap this up in the morning by answering any questions you may have. Dinner should be within the hour. Gentlemen, I'll meet you at the ambulance. It shouldn't take too long to load it up. So, shall we all gather in the dinning room, at let's say, six o'clock!"

Everyone got up from their seats, started stretching and gathering up their things and taking them to their rooms. After dinner, they gathered in the study and had a round of drinks.

Edward asked Felmen, "Have you had a chance to talk to Julius about my parents?"

Felmen said, "No, I haven't, but I'll do it now."

"Edward said, "Thank you. I'll try to contact them once again."

Edward received a message that the phone had been disconnected! Not wanting to wait until Felmen and Julius finished their conversation, he approached them and said, "I tried calling home, but I received a message the phone has been disconnected. I can't understand what is going on." Looking at Felmen he asked, "Do you think maybe they have been arrested because of my involvement with you on the train? They know my last name and I am sure they have figured out by now I am with you!"

Julius answered for Felmen and said, "This could very well be, but they would only have them in for questioning. They would not have the telephone disconnected. That would be the last thing they would do, especially if they were hoping you would call so they could get information on your whereabouts. I don't want to concern you Edward, but let's figure the worst. They could have been sent into the Ghetto. I'll have our people check it out. Give me the address. What's your father's first name?"

"232 Kapuuziner Str. Dusseldorf . My fathers first name is Joseph," said Edward.

Julius took a pad from his inside jacket pocket and jotted down the information.

Edward walked over to the patio door and motioned for Sylvia to go out on the patio with him. Sylvia stepped out onto the patio just ahead of Edward. She turned and saw the concerned look on his face.

Edward looked back toward the door and not seeing anyone said, "I know we are not to discuss the plans, but have you made up your mind yet if you are going along with their plans?"

She hesitated for a moment and answered him, "Yes, I believe I am. What about you?"

"I am as well, but let me say this first. There is no one I would rather have going along with me than you, but I am concerned about your safety. Julius is checking on my parents and sisters whereabouts. I am not sure I can pull this off myself with all my concerns focusing on my family, and now you. I am sure you are concerned about your grandmother and aunt and I just hope you know what you are doing. You know, we have known each other for such a short time, but I am beginning to have special feelings for you and I hope you have for me," said Edward.

"I do," Sylvia said as she gave Edward a kiss on the cheek. She added, "We had better go back in now."

Felmen saw his daughter and Edward coming back into the house and motioned for them to join him and Julius.

"Having second thoughts, are we?" Julius asked as he poured a glass of wine for himself and asked if they cared to join him.

They both agreed and Edward added, "That's yes to the drinks, not the second thoughts. That is, if I can speak for the both of us?"

Sylvia nodded in agreement. "Good then," Julius said, "We want you to be comfortable in your decision. I will be the first to admit this is a very dangerous assignment, but very possible to perform."

Felmen finished his drink and said, "This has been a long day. I believe we all should retire and try to get a good night's rest. In the morning you will be experiencing a breakfast fit for a king.

You will be getting what Julius calls his famous, Matzoh and Mushroom Omelet."

With that everyone got up and headed for their rooms. Edward walked Sylvia to her room, gave her a good night kiss, and said, "I hope I did not frighten you with my concerns."

"No, you did not. I know the hazards we face, but I feel together and with the help of the others, we can pull it off."

Edward held her in his arms and kissed her on the forehead as if he were kissing a child and said, "Everything will be all right. Get a good night's rest and I'll see you in the morning."

5

Edward was running a bit late for breakfast and joined the others in the dining room. He dished himself up one of Julius's famous Matzoh and mushroom omelet, asking, "Did I hear the phone ringing earlier this morning?"

Julius answered, "Yes you did. It was Preben with information about your parents and sisters."

"What did he say? Are they all right?" Edward asked as he placed his napkin down along side his plate and leaned toward Julius to hear better.

"They seem to have avoided being arrested by the Gestapo. Otto, your friend from the train, called the house asking all kinds of questions about you, Felmen, and Sylvia. Your father was smart enough to know what was next. Your father had the phone disconnected and closed up the house so it would appear there was no one living there. Preben suspected this and had his people watch the house. When your Father was seen coming out of the house before daylight, Preben's people followed him and explained where you were and that they would help get him and the rest of the family to you. Preben insisted they take the first available train out of Dusseldorf to Nuremburg, where they would be taken off the train and transported here where proper documentation and arrangements could be made for them to be taken into Switzerland. And if all goes well, they should be here later today," said Julius.

You could see the relief on Edward's face as he reached over and placed another of Julius's famous, Matzoh and mushroom omelets on his plate. Sylvia's face was gleaming after hearing the good news.

Julius didn't want to get every ones hopes up, so he said, "We are not out of the woods yet people. We still have to get them here and complete their documentation packages. I believe Louis; you have completed all your photographs for our group of four, correct?"

Louis answered, "Yes, I have. Do you want me to stay and do the others when they arrive?"

"Yes, stick around and take care of the photos. I'll have someone start working up their documentation packages. They should be completed and delivered here by the time they arrive." As he finished off the coffee, Julius said, "Bring your coffee with you," and added, "if anyone is in need of medical treatment from eating my cooking please see our resident Doctor, Captain Kurt Von Mueller!"

Edward laughed and said, "Thank you Julius. Thank you for everything!" Edward's eyes started to tear up and he became choked up and could not speak.

Sylvia walked around the table, put her arms around him, and said, "Everything is going to work out just fine."

Everyone was getting settled in the study as Julius walked to the front of the room and stood next to the artist easel. "I believe we have now covered everyone. I would like to address a couple more items with Edward," Julius said as he started flipping through the charts, until he came to a chart marked Mauthausen Concentration Camp.

Julius pointed out an area marked as the Russian Camp Hospital and said, "Edward, you will request an area in the main compound for your experiments. You must insist on having your own facilities and they shall be off limits to all camp personnel, with the exceptions of the Commandant. Familiarize yourselves with the layout of the compound. Your medical facility should be located in a way that you will have a clear view of the coming and going of all prisoners. Here is a layout of the medical facility for you to give to the commandant. You will be provided with outside support. We will contact you, you are not to try to contact any one on the outside. We will also provide you with an emergency contact. Only, in a life or death situation, shall they be contacted! Other than the ambulance all of your vehicle needs will be furnished by the camp's motor pool. Aurek, you will do all the driving and at no time will the nurses be called upon to drive. For that matter, they will never be required to leave or be left alone in the medical facility without a male being present."

A couple of hours had passed when there was a light tap at the study door. Louis opened the door, stuck his head in, and asked, "Can anyone use a fresh cup of coffee?"

"Good timing, Louis," Julius said and added, "Okay, let's take a break people. Be back in fifteen minutes."

"I know I can use a cup," Felmen said, as he placed his cup under the spout on the large silver coffee urn Louis had set on a side table.

"Well, I see we are all back now so let's get into the question and answer phase. I will start with you, Edward. I noticed you have been taking lots of notes. I hope they are not all questions."

Edward smiled and answered, "Only a couple." He looked

down at his notebook and said, "You said we had free reign of the camp. What exactly do you mean by that?"

Julius answered by saying, "No one in Camp Mauthausen is going to question the orders of Heinrich Himmler. His actual phone number is on the orders. You can even invite the commandant to call him personally. I guarantee you he will not make the call. Especially now that he has just recently been assigned to Mauthausen and promoted to Colonel. So when I say you will have free reign of the camp, I mean no one is going to question your authority. You will be able to request most anything you require to make you and your staff comfortable."

Edward nodded in agreement with Julius's answer and asked, "What about any type of relationships between my staff and the personnel of the camp?"

Julius answered, "There should be absolutely none. The records of both ladies show they are married. Sylvia, what is your husband's name?"

"Theodore," Sylvia answered.

"And yours Ethel?" Julius asked.

Ethel answered, "Walter, my husband of eight years."

"Edward, Aurek is single like you. It will be your responsibility to keep both your staff and the camp staff in line in regards to relationships. Again, I remind you, at no time will the young ladies be alone. As officers I am sure you will be invited to dinner with the other camp Officers. You should attend, but do not discuss any of the testing you are involved in. We are waiting until after the holidays before having you report to the commandant. The reason for this is we don't want any one meeting you before they go home for holiday leave and possibly mentioning you to others on the outside. The less anyone on the outside knows about you and your operation the better," said Julius.

The question and answer section lasted most of the day. Julius checked his watch and said, "Well, now that we have all your questions answered I guess we can safely say the operations briefing is over. Until it's time for you to depart I believe it would be advantageous for you to study and memorize all there is to know about your character."

They could hear the sounds of muffled voices coming from the foyer and heard the big front door slam. There was a knock at the study door and a voice said, "This is Preben, anyone home? The Weinsteins are here."

Edward jumped to his feet, ran across the room, and slid the doors wide open. He moved past Preben, hugged his mother with one arm, reached out to grab his father's arm, pulling him into his chest and said, "Mama, Papa, I am so sorry about everything. I know I am responsible for you having to leave our home and your business Papa."

Edward's mother said, as she and Edward's father both patted him on the back, "We are just thankful you are safe Edward. I don't know what we would have done if we had lost you." Edward saw his two sisters standing there with tears running down their cheeks. He let go of his mother and father, grabbed his sisters and gave them a big hug and told them he was so happy to see them all. There was not a dry eye in the house.

Edward said, "Everyone, this is my mother, father, and two sisters." They went around the room so each person could introduce him or herself to the Weinsteins.

Julius said, with a voice of authority, "I believe we should all leave Edward and his family to themselves, so they can catch up on family news."

Edward said, "If it is all the same, I would like Sylvia to remain."

Julius said, "But, of course," and motioned for Sylvia to have a seat. He pulled the doors closed as he left the room.

"Well, where do we begin?" Edward asked.

Papa spoke first by saying, "We are thankful this young man, Otto, made the mistake of calling us first. I knew we didn't have much time before the Gestapo would be there in person asking questions."

"Why did you have the telephone disconnected?" Edward asked.

Edward's father replied, "I don't know. I thought maybe they would think we had moved. I am not used to all this. As Preben's people explained to us, you were with Mr. Felmen and his daughter and we had to leave Dusseldorf right away. I recognized the name Felmen, as that is the name the young man, Otto, kept asking me about. Thank God for men like Preben. If not for him and his people, there's no telling what would have happened to us. Preben has informed us that you have joined the resistance movement, is this true?"

Edward held Sylvia's hand and said, "Yes, both Sylvia and I have agreed to an assignment that we are not at liberty to discuss at this time. I will say this; I will not be going to Switzerland with the family but will join you later. Mr. Felmen's mother and sister have been picked up and sent to a Ghetto. Julius and his people are working on getting them out of the Ghetto and into Switzerland before they are sent to a work camp."

Edward's mother asked, "How long will it be before you can join us?"

Edward squeezed Sylvia's hand and answered his mother's question by saying, "Not too long. Sylvia was going with her Father, but things have changed a bit. You all must be exhausted. Why don't you let us take you to your rooms so you can refresh yourselves and take a short nap before dinner."

Sylvia said, as she stood and ushered them out the door,

"Julius assigned the rooms this morning when we heard you were coming."

Edward showed his mother and father to their room and Sylvia took the girls to theirs. After dinner, everyone gathered in the study.

Julius said, as he entered the room, "We will continue by processing the Weinstein family tonight. We have all the necessary paperwork and just need to send you down for photos. We will start with you Dorothy, then Iris, and then Mr. Weinstein and Mrs. Weinstein. Please go over the paperwork I am handing out and memorize your name, address and telephone number. You most likely will not be asked, but just in case. We must act quickly on getting you out of Germany; therefore you will be departing in the morning. There is a medical conference being held in Bern, Switzerland, December twenty-first. You and your family have signed papers authorizing you to travel there. You and your wife will travel together and Dorothy and Iris will travel alone. We can't take the chance of you all being together, as they could be looking for a man and his wife with two adult daughters. Of course, you will not be attending the conference. Someone will meet you and your daughters on the train once you are in Switzerland. From there, you may go where you please. It will be too dangerous for you to notify Edward of your whereabouts. He will find out in due time."

For the rest of the evening everyone visited with one another.

Louis entered the room and asked, "Is there a Mr. and Mrs. Plate here?"

Edward's Father stood and said, "Yes, here we are!" Everyone laughed.

Edward said, "We could have used you in the play Papa."

Dorothy and Iris received their papers also. Felmen held his glass up, motioned for everyone to gather around so he could pour drinks, and said, "Edward has something he would like to say."

"I would like to take this opportunity to thank Julius, Preben, and their people for all they are doing for us. And Mr. Felmen, I know where your heart is at this moment and hear you are working tirelessly on getting others taken care of. May God bless you all richly for your thoughtfulness of others."

Edward's father stood and said, " Here, Here!"

A while later Edward noticed his father had nodded off. He reached over, took the glass out of his father's hand and set it on the table next to him and said, "Come on Papa. It's time for bed."

Edward's mother got up and took her husband's hand and said, as they left the room, "Take care all. We will see you in the morning."

Julius reminded them he would be waking them at six a.m.

The next morning Louis, Sylvia, and Ethel had fixed breakfast and everyone was making small talk, dreading the good byes that were coming. Aurek and Preben had already loaded the luggage into the cars.

Julius said, as he gulped down his coffee, "Well, we must do it. Mr. and Mrs. Weinstein, Aurek will take you in the first car. Dorothy, you and Iris will be going with Preben in about ten minutes."

Edward said good bye to them all, took a step back upon the porch, and wrapped his arm around Sylvia waist. He bent over, looked into the back window, and said to his mother and father, "See you before long. Do take care!"

Dorothy and Iris said their good byes and got into the car with Preben. Before they drove away, Julius said to Preben, "See you and Aurek back here in the morning. Be careful!"

Preben said, "Thank you. We will," and drove away.

Edward said, "I think I'll go inside and study for a while."

Sylvia thought to herself how hard this must be on Edward.

She knew she would have to go through it with her father when they were ready to leave after the holidays.

It was January fifth, 1939, and Julius told everyone to give him their notebooks so he could destroy them for safety reasons. He also informed Felmen he would be leaving for Switzerland in the morning with Preben. Edward, Sylvia, and the others would be leaving for Mauthausen today.

Edward's stomach rolled over when he heard Julius say it, even though he knew it would be coming. He looked at Sylvia and the others and he could tell by their expressions they felt the same. Like opening night jitters he thought.

All of the notebooks were lying on a table in the study and everyone was in uniform. Aurek pulled the ambulance up to the front door.

Edward shook Felmen and Julius's hand and thanked them for everything. He got into the ambulance with Aurek and Ethel to give Sylvia time to say a proper goodbye to her father.

Felmen told his daughter everything was going to be all right and that Julius had told him her Grandmother and Aunt Glory were already on their way to Switzerland.

"I know you are in good hands with Edward and he will take care of you. We will see you all in Switzerland soon," said Felmen.

Sylvia climbed into the ambulance, sat next to Ethel, and laid her head on her shoulder. Ethel put her arm around Sylvia, told her it would be okay, and she would see him again soon.

6

After having only driven for about three and one half-hours, they pulled up to the front gate of Mauthausen. Edward reached out and handed the guard his papers. The guard snapped to attention and told the other guard standing there to call the Commandant. He instructed Aurek to pull the vehicle up in front of the building, where another soldier stood waving.

Aurek stopped the vehicle in front of a sign, SS-Hauptsturmfuehrer Wiesbaden. Edward got out and walked up on the porch, as Lukas was coming out the door to meet him.

Lukas Wiesbaden was a tall, well-built man in his mid thirties. His uniform fit like a glove and you could see his rank insignia of colonel had recently been sewn onto the fading uniform.

After a couple of heil Hitler's, Lukas invited Edward inside and said, "Have your staff join us."

Edward turned and motioned for Aurek and the others to join him inside. Edward introduced the others to Colonel Wiesbaden. "This is Lieutenant Bamberger," said Edward, as Ethel snapped to attention. "And this is Lieutenant Vulkan and Lieutenant Borg," said Edward, as both Sylvia and Aurek joined Ethel standing at attention.

Lukas told them to sit down and ordered his clerk to bring coffee and mugs into his office. He looked over the orders and said, "This is odd. Reichsfuhrer Himmler was just here no more than two weeks ago on an inspection and he made no mention of this program."

Edward was taken back for a moment, but said, "I believe Doctor Joseph Mengele chose Mauthausen."

"He has never been to Mauthausen. Plus we have our own onsite medical staff," Lukas said, as he motioned for the clerk to enter and pointed to the small table next to his desk for him to place the tray of coffee and mugs.

Edward said, "Maybe that is why Himmler was here to inspect your facilities. On the request of Doctor Mengele. As for your medical staff, they will continue to provide you and your staff with medical assistance. We are assigned to perform tests and evaluations on the prisoners."

"Yes, that is very possible. We are always the last to know," said Lukas.

Lukas finished looking over the orders, handed them back to Edward, and said, "Very well then, Captain. What is it that I can do for you?"

Edward stood and walked over to a window. He saw a building next to the main gate and asked, "Is building 557 being used for anything at the present time?"

Lukas got up, joined Edward at the window, and said, "Yes, it's our Ration breakdown point!"

"Is there a possibility for me to have that building for my medical facility?" Edward asked, as he returned to his seat.

"Is there any reason for you to have that building? Couldn't any of the others work for you?" Lukas asked, as he poured Edward a cup of coffee.

"No, I need a facility that is not within the compound. We need a place away from the prisoners and I might add the medical facilities will be off limits to all personnel, with the exception of you and your deputy," answered Edward.

"Very well. I'll have them start moving out today. It will take a couple of days if you are expecting quarters as well."

"Yes I am," said Edward.

"We can put you and Lieutenant Borg with our staff officers, but we do not have any facilities for the women. I guess we could clear out one of the barracks for a couple of nights until we have your medical facilities completed," said Lukas.

Edward stated, "I will require four private rooms with bathing facilities for me and my staff. Also, I'll need up to six additional rooms for patients, with a minimum of two baths," as he handed Lukas a drawing of what he wanted.

"Do you realize how much this is going to cost and how long this may take? This is Mauthausen, a Class III Camp. Not Hitler's Roost at Birches Garden! Since the orders are counter signed by SS-Reichsfuhrer Heinrich Himmler, I wonder if maybe he is allocating funds for this project," asked Lukas.

"I wasn't told he was, but maybe you should call him and inquire," Edward responded.

"No, that won't be necessary. Why don't you and you staff get settled in and come back here for dinner around six o'clock. I'll introduce you to my staff," said Lukas.

He walked them to the door and ordered the clerk to close down barracks 236 and have the men moved over to barrack 237. Lukas hoped this was only a couple of weeks as he ordered, "Have Sergeant Bothmann take a detail over and help move the residents out."

Edwards added, "Have a guard detail assigned to barrack 236 until the medical facilities are completed."

"Yes, do that also!" Lukas agreed.

Later that evening, at dinner, Lukas introduced Edward and his staff to the camp staff. Captain Malzmueller, a man that appeared to spend too much time in the mess hall and must have tipped the scales at close to two hundred and fifty pounds, approached Edward and said, "I understand Captain Von Mueller, you've instructed Corporal Haeberle to post guards at barracks 236. Well, I am the Captain of the guards and I will instruct the guards to their assignments."

Edward replied, "Well, did Corporal Haeberle inform you the commandant agreed with my instructions? He felt as I do, for the ladies safety, there should be guards posted. So as long as you are in charge of the guards, I am informing you there will be guards posted at each entrance of the barracks. Maybe you would like to discuss this with Hauptsturmfuehrer Wiesbaden?"

The vein in Captain Malzmueller's forehead looked as if it was going to burst as he turned and walked away without answering Edward.

Lukas did not hear the conversation between Edward and Captain Malzmueller, as he was more concerned about entertaining Sylvia and Ethel.

Edward also met the camp doctor, Major Hanh. He was a much older man than Edward. In fact, Edward was surprised to see someone that old still in the service, especially in the medical field. He was glad Hanh was older because he wouldn't know any of the doctors that Edward supposedly studied under; therefore there were no questions about Edward's background. Edward felt it was time for them to call it a night, so gave the sign to Sylvia and Ethel. He walked over to Lukas and said, "It has been a long day and I believe it is time to escort the ladies to their quarters."

Lukas said, "I understand. Good night ladies. See you in the morning and please join me for breakfast. You too, Captain Von Mueller," he added.

Walking back to their quarters, Edward waited until they were in an isolated area before he said, "Well, I certainly got off to a good start with Captain Malzmueller."

"The Commandant didn't seem to hear your conversation or just didn't pay any attention to it. He was more interested in talking to Ethel and me," Sylvia said.

"Yes, I noticed," Edward replied. "Well, here we are. Good night ladies. See you in the morning."

He turned and joined Aurek walking up the hill to their barracks.

The next morning, after breakfast, Lukas took them on a tour of the camp. He took them down into the quarry. There they saw where prisoners were forced to run up the 186 steps out of the stone quarry carrying heavy boulders. These were the stairs of death Julius had told them about.

Lukas took them back up to the main compound area and as they were walking by the Russian camp he asked Edward, "Would you like to see their hospital?"

"Not at this time," Edward answered.

It took everything in their power to control their emotions. Lukas proudly exhibited the crematoria saying, "Well, they work in the quarry until they are no longer useful to us and then they have a nice long shower," as he laughed.

Sylvia knew she had to get out of there right then and asked Lukas, "Do you think the small town we drove through on the way here has a store where I could pick up a few needed things?"

"I am sure they do. Take my driver," Lukas answered.

Edward spoke up and said, "Lieutenant Borg can drive us.

I would like to check the town out, also. I am sure the others would, too."

They all agreed that would be fine. Lukas seemed to be disappointed the tour had to end, but instructed Aurek to go to the motor pool and sign out a car.

On their way into town, Edward pointed to his left and said to Aurek, "See that road, with the sign and arrows pointing to the river? Let's take it, okay?"

Aurek followed the road to the end. Edward said, "Pull over here and let's get out for a while."

They were parked at the water's edge of the beautiful Danube River. It was hard to believe that such horrifying things were going on just up the road from this peaceful place.

Edward remarked, "Can you believe this? Look at the water, look at this place, and how peaceful it is. This is going to be the place where we can come when we need to get away from that despicable place."

They all agreed. They did not know how long they could stand up to the stress of knowing what was going on. There was nothing they could do, but take out six prisoners a month.

After two weeks, the medical facility was ready to be moved into. Edward assigned the two girls rooms on the end of the building, where they would have their own entrance. Edward and Aurek would be on the other end, where they also would have their own entrance. There were six smaller rooms and one large examining room in the center with bathing facilities for both men and women. Edward and the others were surprised with all the cooperation they were getting from Lukas. Julius was correct in saying they would have free reign.

Edward asked Lukas for a couple of men to help unload the ambulance. "Have them report to Lieutenant Borg. Thank you," he stated.

The girls were putting away the medical supplies, when a young soldier knocked on the front door and asked for Captain Von Mueller.

Sylvia said, "I believe he is with the Commandant."

"We have the supplies and medical equipment he ordered. Where do you want them?" asked the soldier.

Sylvia and Ethel both knew Edward hadn't ordered any supplies.

Sylvia said, "Bring them in here," as she stepped back out of the way.

She looked outside and saw Aurek helping unload the truck and low and behold there was Louis in a German uniform. Edward was leaving the Commandant's office and noticed the truck backed up to the porch. He saw Aurek and a few men unloading equipment, but did not recognize Louis until he went to step up on the porch and almost lost his footing.

Louis spoke right up and said, "Here are the medical supplies and equipment you ordered, Sir!"

Going into the building he asked, in a low voice, "How is everything going?"

"Fine so far. We are just getting into our facilities and I have not had a chance to work with any of the prisoners," Edward answered.

Louis told Edward, "Once you have chosen six prisoners, we will need their measurements, along with their head size. I'll pick them up on my next trip." He added, "I have good news for you and Sylvia. Your parents and sisters, as well as Sylvia's Grandmother and Aunt are all doing fine in Switzer . . ." Before he could finish, he saw a German Officer coming in the door and in a loud voice said, "Sign here sir and we will be on our way."

Edward turned and saw Lukas standing there looking at some of the equipment. He looked around and walked over to one of the restrooms marked women and opened the door to look inside. "Very nice," he said, as he walked up to Ethel. "Are your quarters adequate, Lieutenant Bamberger?" Lukas asked.

"Yes, Sir. They are, thank you," replied Ethel.

As Louis and the other men got into the truck and drove out of the compound, Edward said, "Okay people, let's get ourselves organized and make this place look like a medical facility."

Lukas took the hint and said, "When you are ready to pick your first group of prisoners Captain Von Mueller, let me know and I'll have a roll call."

After Lukas left, Edward was able to tell Sylvia the good news of her family.

"It was certainly good to see Louis. Too bad we were interrupted by Lukas. I hope he is not going to be a problem. Are you going to be able to handle him?" Edward asked Ethel.

"Yes, I believe so. I'll let you know when I can't," replied Ethel.

The hardest part of this assignment was coming up. Lukas had all the prisoners standing outside in the roll call area and Edward had to pick six of them. He had thought about it for some time and figured he would pick the youngest, for they had so much to live for. Then there were the older ones who couldn't stand much more pain and suffering. What to do? He decided he would go by family names and if there were not enough to account for six in one family he would choose a couple families, with one or two or even three children for a total of six prisoners.

He asked Lukas, "Do you have a roster listing family names?"

Lukas said to the officer standing next to him, "Give me the roster listing the families by name." The Officer shuffled through the rosters, came to the correct one, and handed it to the Commandant.

"Here," said Lukas, as he handed it on to Edward.

It was so cold and Edward shivered as he flipped through the pages of the roster. He saw the name Cohen with the number 6 beside it.

He yelled out, "Cohen, Amiel, Ailat, Hadar, Miriam, Molly and Meira Cohen! Front and center."

The groups of prisoners were separated by sex, with the exception of the children, the boys were with their mothers if they were younger than fourteen. There was a lot of relaying of the names. Edward could see a man and a boy of eighteen or so walking toward the stand he was standing on; following behind them were four females. Edward couldn't imagine what must have been going through their minds.

Lukas had turned the formation over to his deputy and gone inside where it was warm. Edward took the Cohen family to the medical facility. On their way to the facility they could not resist hugging each other. They were all crying, but these were tears of joy. When they were inside Sylvia, Ethel, and Aurek set-up a processing line. Aurek made medical records for each of them. Sylvia weighed each family member and Ethel did a quick exam. They were asked to shower and were issued clean clothes.

Edward showed them their rooms and said, "You will remain in your room until told otherwise. As you can see, we have set-up a couple of tables here in the examining room; you will be taking all your meals here."

Mr. Cohen asked Edward, "What is going to happen to my family and me?"

Edward answered, "We will be performing some minor test on you and your family. They are nothing to worry about, I assure you."

Edward wanted to take them all in his arms, hug them, and tell them what was really happening. He wanted them to know they were on their way to Switzerland, but he knew he couldn't do that.

Edward told the others, while the Cohen's were in their rooms, "I don't know how we are going to stall for thirty days before we can take this family to Stuttgart. We have to work out a better plan. I wish I could talk to Julius."

Aurek asked, "Did you tell the commandant the schedule for the evaluation of the prisoners?"

"No, I did not. I only told him I wanted to see six prisoners at a time. I am not sure he even knows about the evaluations period. I will feel him out at dinner tonight," Edward answered.

Mr. Cohen knocked on his door from the inside and waited until someone answered it. Sylvia heard the knock and explained, "You do not have to knock to get out of your room."

"But the Doctor said to remain in our room until told otherwise," Mr. Cohen said.

"That's okay. If any of you have to go to the bathroom just go, but return to your room afterwards. He does not want you sitting around in the examining room," said Sylvia.

"I have a question then," Mr. Cohen said. "Can our family visit with each other in one room?"

Answering for Edward, Sylvia said, "Of course you can." The tears of joy overflowed from Mr. Cohen's eyes and ran down his cheeks.

Sylvia turned away before Mr. Cohen saw her tears. Sylvia had Aurek get the other family members and put them into Mr. Cohen's room. It was a bit crowded, but that did not bother the Cohen family one bit.

Edward ordered all the patients meals from the German kitchen and informed the mess officer his patients would eat the same food as the camp staff.

At dinner, Edward asked Lukas if he had heard about the

prisoner's evaluation conference held in Stuttgart. He purposely did not mention any dates or schedules.

"No I haven't, what is that all about?" asked Lukas.

"We are to take the prisoners there twice a month for evaluation. They of course, don't get to enjoy the round trip," Edward answered, as he and Lukas laughed. Edward thought he was going to be sick. The only reason he did not, was the fact that he knew the outcome for these prisoners was freedom, not death.

The next day, Edward told Ethel to administer the first shots. He said to the others, "Lukas knows nothing about the evaluation conferences; therefore we are going to move up the date by two weeks. I'll get in touch with Julius tonight."

"But he said to do that only in a life or death situation," Sylvia said.

"This is! We are going to double the count and save twelve prisoners, not only six per month," replied Edward.

Edward said to Aurek, "Get a car from the motor pool. I'll drive it into town to make my call. I would tell Lukas I was going to town for some fun, but I am afraid he would want to join me."

Edward drove through town to use the telephone so not to be seen by anyone from camp on their way into town.

7

Julius was not happy with Edward at first, but agreed with Edward that it was worth a try.

He said to Edward, "Write this down. When arriving from the south, take A9 to Munich. At the end of the highway, follow the signs to Mittlerer Ring Ost. You will drive through two tunnels and then turn right at Tocher Park. Then enter Ifflandstrasse and continue straight. At Maximillanstrasse, turn right, go to second drive way on right, and pull to the back of the house. When you leave, you can get out by going straight through to the next street. Stop only long enough to drop off your passengers. Someone will be there to meet you on the first of February. Commit that information to memory and destroy what you wrote it on right away. If there are any changes, you will be notified by Louis with your next shipment of medical supplies."

"Thanks!" said Edward, as he hung up the receiver and went back to the car. He sat for a few minutes and memorized the direction. He then found a box of matches in the glove compartment and burned the directions.

Back at camp, Edward had Aurek take the car back to the

motor pool and told him to reserve a car for the first of February. He doesn't have to tell Aurek why.

Aurek smiled and said, "Yes, Sir."

Sylvia and Ethel were happy about the news, also. Only three more days and they would have the first of many, they hoped, on their road to freedom. The shots were taking effect quite well. The Cohen family just sat in their rooms and stared at the walls.

Edward said, "We should get the Cohens out on display." He instructed Aurek to take them out into the exercise yard that had been added to the rear of the medical facility. The Germans could see the patients being led by Aurek around in a circle. They looked like a bunch of zombies and that was exactly what Edward and the others wanted them to believe.

On the first of February, Aurek was up early and picked up a car for Edward and the girls. He would be driving the ambulance and his passengers would be incoherent for most of the day. The best part would be when they came to and actually found out what was really going on in their lives. Edward decided to have Ethel ride with Aurek to attend to the Cohen family.

Lukas was out on the porch and waved for Edward to come over to him. Edward thought, "Now what?" as he walked over to salute and greet Lukas.

"Good morning, Sir," Edward said, as he put on his gloves.

Lukas asked, "Would you prefer one of my men drive you to Stuttgart?"

"No. That won't be necessary, but thank you for the offer," Edward replied as he saluted and turned to walk away.

As he got into the car Edward said, "That was close. Lukas offered us a driver."

Sylvia wrapped a blanket around her legs and asked, "What would you have done if he insisted?"

"I am not sure. We will have to face that if, and when, it ever happens," said Edward.

Edward drove the car out the gate with Aurek close behind. It was getting dark when they pulled onto Ifflandstrasse.

Edward said, "Not too much farther now. Keep your eyes open for Maximillianstrasse."

Sylvia pointed to the street sign and said, "This is it."

Edward knowing it was just around the corner, pulled over and told Sylvia, "Let's go say our good byes to the Cohen family."

Aurek had pulled up right behind the car. He got out, walked to the back of the ambulance, opened up both back doors, and asked Ethel to turn on the over head light. Edward and Sylvia joined Aurek and looked inside at the Cohens.

Edward said, "How do you feel Mr. Cohen?"

"Fine. What's going on?" Mr. Cohen asked. "Is everyone else all right?"

They all said, at the same time, "We're fine."

Edward explained to them that they were on their way to Switzerland. He apologized that they were in a stupor for a few days, but told them that was the only way they could convince the Germans the test they were performing was working.

"Sit tight and we will be dropping you off just around the corner," said Edward.

Mr. Cohen reached out, grabbed Edward's hand, and said, "God bless you and your people. You have been so kind to my family and me. You, you are Camp Angels!"

Everyone was reaching out, touching each other's hands and crying, and saying, "Thank you. Thank you."

"I expect you are all hungry. There are sandwiches and beverages here in this blue case," Edward said, as he shut the doors to the ambulance.

After dropping the Cohen family off, they proceeded through

the back ally to the street and headed back to camp. Edward reached, took Sylvia's hand, and said, "We haven't had much time for this," as he held her hand up and gripped it.

She said, "No. There hasn't been. I wish I could slide over next to you, but I know we can't take that chance."

Edward put her hand up to his lips and kissed the back of her hand tenderly.

The Cohen family was ushered into the basement by a young man and told someone would be taking photos of them once they had changed into their civilian clothes. He handed them each a card and said, "Memorize the name and address on the card. This is your new identification." Lewis had passed on the measurements for each one of them earlier in the month. There was a hair piece for each of them also.

A couple of the make-up artists who had worked for Felmen in his plays were now working for Julius. They not only brought along their experience, but also all their equipment. They could make a person appear to have a disfigured face so when they were questioned at the border the guard would pass them on through; anything to get rid of them. The burn victim was very effective. One of the make-up artists was having trouble with the Cohen parents, as they could not stop crying.

Ganit, the man in charge, said, "This might work to our benefit. The family has papers allowing them to attend a funeral in a small village, just inside the border, for their twenty-two year old daughter."

Ganit said to the young man that ushered the Cohens into the basement, "Sachiel, you will be traveling along with the Cohens as the priest who will perform the service."

He explained to the Cohens that they were only two and one half-hours from Buchs, Switzerland. Sachiel would be taking them there by car.

"We would normally have you take the train, but your papers show you are from Stuttgart and are only crossing over for the day and returning the next day," said Ganit.

The Cohen's oldest son was going as a burn victim since he was 18 years old and otherwise would be in the German Army.

"Sachiel will explain to the border crossing guards that the daughter you are supposedly burying was in the same fire as your son, but did not make it. Even the most callus person would have compassion for you and your family," Ganit said, as he helped Mrs. Cohen with her coat.

Every one was ready and said their goodbyes to Ganit and his people.

"Please tell the ones at Camp Mauthausen thank you very much. We owe them our lives and we will call them "Camp Angels" forever," Mr. Cohen said, as he stepped into the car.

Another fifteen days had past and they were taking out a couple with two children and a man and his wife. They stopped at a different place this time to say their goodbyes. When they returned to camp they received an invitation to attend a dinner party at the Commandant's quarters. The time was just right, as they would pick another six prisoners the following day; therefore they could all attend. Edward did not want Captain Malzmueller to have to furnish guards for his patients.

Dinner and the conversation was going along fine until Captain Malzmueller, the captain of the guard, said, "Captain Von Mueller. Your patients are eating better than any of the guards. I don't understand why you can't just pick six prisoners out of the gas chamber line and do what ever you do to them."

Edward got to his feet and said, "Captain Malzmueller, I do not have to defend my actions on how I treat any of my patients to you. May I suggest you personally place a call to Doctor Joseph Mengele or Himmler himself and tell them you are not satisfied with the way they have directed Captain Kurt Von Mueller to perform the required tests and evaluations at Mauthausen. That you believe the prisoners picked for these tests should be starved to death. I do not attempt to tell you how to run your guards and I would appreciate it you would do the same when it comes to me or my staff. I really don't see any difference between the results of your methods and mine. I feed them well, then kill them and you work and starve them to death!"

"Enough!" yelled the commandant as he slammed down his fist on the table. "You both will apologize to one another and I never want to hear this type of conversation between you and my staff officers again."

Edward offered his hand for Captain Malzmueller to shake and said, "I apologize captain, but you must understand, the tests we are performing on these prisoners require they be fit. The results are meaningless if they are weak and sick."

Malzmueller said, "Yes. I do understand captain and had no right to say what I said. Let me pour you a drink."

Lukas stood and said, "That's more like it. Let's have some music." He walked over to a Victrola, gave it a few cranks, and checked out some records. He found one by Marlene Detrich and said, "Lili Marlene. This should be a great one."

You could see the confrontation between Captain Malzmueller and Captain Von Mueller made the others uncomfortable. After the music started and Captain Malzmueller poured Captain Von Mueller a drink, it was obvious everyone felt better and they seemed to enjoy themselves for the remainder of the evening.

Even though it appeared Lukas had quite a bit to drink, he behaved himself and left the woman alone. Edward was glad there was no room for dancing because he was sure Lukas would have been all over Ethel.

The next morning Edward stopped by the commandant's office to pick up the family name roster.

The clerk said, "SS-Hauptsturmfuehrer Wiesbaden left camp early this morning and will not return until late this afternoon."

Edward was surprised Lukas could rise so early in the morning after the party the night before and said, "I'll just get the family rosters. I know where they are." As he picked up the stack of rosters Edward noticed a letter addressed to SS-Reichsfuehrer Schmidt. The letter had a note pinned to it that it should be sent that day. The body of the letter contained the following wording:

Lukas Wiesbaden
SS-Hauptsfuehrer Mauthausen

Esteemed Reichsfuhrer!

02.24.39

As you know, the same gas-vans being used in Lanz and Dachau could be used here in Mauthausen since the 'invalid transports' terminate in the special chambers anyway. I wondered if it would be possible to test the effects of our combat gases, in these gas-vans, using the persons who are destined for the chambers.

The only reports available so far are for experiments on animals or of accidents in the manufacturing of the gases. We have Captain Kurt Von Mueller and his staff who could carry out this assignment. Captain Von Mueller is the doctor assigned here to do the tests and experiments with the brain deterioration drug. He has just returned from the Stuttgart evaluation conference. Please advise.

SS-Hauptsturmfuehrer Lukas Wiesbaden Mauthausen

The clerk asked from the outer office, "Did you find the roster, Sir?"

"Yes," Edward said, as he put the letter under the family rosters and walked out of the commandant's office.

The clerk asked, "Do you want me to ask the Deputy to have a roll call formation, Sir?"

"No. I want to look over this roster first," Edward said, as he shut the front door.

Edward showed the letter to Aurek and the girls and said, "We can't let this letter go through. The problem is, if Lukas does not receive an answer, he will most likely send another letter. Although, he may be smart enough to know if SS-Reichsfuehrer Schmidt does not answer him, he had better leave well enough alone."

All the prisoners were assembled in the roll call area. Edward stood and held the microphone in his hand, looked out over the crowd, and thought if only he could put a stop to the senseless killing and set them all free.

"Hartenstein, Kefir, Nechama, Manuel and Kerem," Edward called. He waited until he saw four people walk toward him and continued calling the two remaining names. "Shanker, Oren and Rona." He saw them step forward from the formation and head his direction. Back at the medical facility it was the same routine. Aurek filled out the paperwork, Sylvia weighed each person, and exams were done by Ethel. After their showers, they were assigned to a room. The couples were allowed to share the same room.

There was a knock at the door. Aurek opened it up and stepped back so the cook could roll the food cart into the examining room. Edward had the patients brought in from their rooms for dinner. He explained to each of them that he knew it had been a long time since they had eaten a balance meal, so they were to take their time eating and not over eat to the point they became sick.

When dinner was finished, the patients were sent back to

their rooms. Edward told Sylvia and the others, “I’m going into town tonight to make contact with Julius. He has to know about the letter.”

Later that night Edward talked to Julius and told him of the letter. Julius was quiet for a moment and then said, “I’ll give it a couple of days for normal mail delivery before I respond. Lukas will receive his answer from Schmidt, but he will not like it.”

Edward was amazed at the network of operators Julius had working for him. They were the size of a small army. It didn’t seem to matter what the situation was; he always had an answer and a plan to address it. He wondered where men like Julius came from. Are they just born leaders?

Edward stopped at the river edge before returning to camp. He could see light from the boats and wondered if the crews on board were aware of the atrocities going on just a few miles away. It was so tranquil here and it was so hard to return to camp after spending any time by the river. He wished he had the others with him, even though there would be no conversation between them while they were here. It would just be nice to have them near.

8

A week had gone by when Lukas received his long awaited letter from Schmidt in the form of a telegram. He opened it up in the outer office and quickly read the first couple of lines as he walked into his office and closed the door. The telegram read:

Headquarters
Of the
State (Political) Police
18 Hinderstrasse, Berlin Germany

03.07.39

My Dear Hauptsturmfuehrer Wiesbaden,
I can only say, you are very fortunate you are still in command of Mauthausen Concentration Camp after such a gross breach of security. If you, in the future, ever mention any aspects of what goes on in your area of responsibility I myself will see to it that you are assigned to the eastern front! To mention places, people's names, and their duties is dereliction of duty.
I can only assume you will forget everything about the letter you sent to me. Please be advised this telegram does not require an answer!

SS- Reichsfuerer Schmidt *2349600/SS-5630 03.07.39*
State (Political) Police Berlin

Lukas crumpled up the telegram, walked over, opened the lid on the potbelly stove, put the telegram into the fire, and watched it burn, along with any hope he might have had for a promotion.

Lukas invited Edward for dinner and asked him to come alone. Edward was surprised, as he always asked for the others to join him. Edward accepted and informed the others that he would be going alone. After dinner, Lukas poured drinks and asked Edward if he ever had any dealings with SS- Reichsfuerer Schmidt?

Edward said, "No. Why do you ask?"

Lukas answered, "Oh, no reason. I was just wondering if you have ever heard of him?"

Edward replied, "Isn't he in charge of the State Police?"

"Yes," Lukas answered, as he handed Edward a drink. "I have heard you don't want to get on his bad side," Lukas added.

Edward couldn't figure out where Lukas was going with the conversation.

Lukas said, "I might as well tell you. I messed up and suggested to Schmidt that the same gas-vans as in Lanz and Dachau could be used here in Mauthausen. I suggested maybe you and your staff could be responsible for the operation. Well, he sent me a telegram and informed me, I was very fortunate that I was still in command of Mauthausen. I had disclosed your name and what research you are performing here. He also said it was a breach of security and a dereliction of duty. I am walking on eggshells here.

Edward asked Lukas, "Why would you think I would want to be responsible for such a task? The task at hand is enough for me."

At least Lukas was honest when he answered, "I figured I would get a promotion out of it. Now I am lucky to still be in command."

Edward said, "But you are still in command and that must mean something." Edward hated flattering Lukas like that and it made him feel sick at his stomach. He wanted to tell him he deserved to be put in the van and gassed, but he didn't. He told

Lukas everything would work out, to just cool it for a while and this would pass.

Edward looked over the family roster and couldn't believe his eyes. He called out for Aurek and explained he would have to make the roll call and pick out the next six prisoners because after checking the names he found the names of Doctor Siegel and his family.

"I can't take the chance I might be recognized. I have to be out of the picture until they have had their shots," Edward said.

Aurek called out the names of Doctor Siegel, his wife, and three daughters.

"Sylvia, try and find out what happened to the Siegel's and how they got here?" said Edward.

Doctor Siegel told Sylvia he and his family were caught at the border and turned into the State Police. They had been assigned to the Ghetto prior to being sent to Mauthausen.

Edward was afraid to make contact with the family. He was concerned that if he did and they were caught they could give him and the others away. He felt it would be better to stay out of the way and let the others handle them all the way through until they were delivered to Ganit and his people.

A couple of months after Edward talked to Lukas about the telegram he said to the others, "We should change our method of picking the prisoners. Now I believe we should save the mothers and their children. I don't have to explain to Lukas what I am doing, especially now. That telegram took the wind out of his sails. He hasn't been the same since."

Edward picked out three mothers with one child each. He looked at the children as they were being processed and thought these little guys should be on a picnic with their parents, not in a death camp. Their little eyes didn't have any emotion showing through at all. After they showered and dressed in clean clothes, they had what Edward thought must be one of the best dinners they had eaten in a long time.

Even though they were being treated well, their mothers were asking why they were there and why they were singled out?

One of the ladies spoke up and said, "We see you taking families out and we never see them again. It's like we see the guards take away the sick, but they never come back. What is going to happen to us and our children?"

So many questions, Edward thought and we just continued to lie to the prisoners. This was getting harder for them, rather than easier. Edward could see by the roster the women's husbands were in the camp.

He made a mental note to choose their three husbands and one mother with two children the next time.

Edward and his group were on their way to drop off the mothers and their children when they came upon a roadblock. They were fortunate; as there were two cars and one military truck ahead of them. Edward went back, talked to Aurek, and checked out the patients. He was sure the drug was wearing off by now and was concerned about how they might act. As he suspected, they were as normal as before they received the shots. Edward took the chance the ladies would understand and not be frightened, as they found themselves in an ambulance with no idea of how they got there.

"Okay ladies. Listen up. I don't have much time to explain. We are going to ship you and your children off to Switzerland. Your husbands will follow soon. So just sit there, don't say a word, and help us make this work. I'll explain more later. Please do not pay any attention to what the driver Aurek says to the guards up ahead. Just sit there and stare at each other," said Edward.

"Ethel, try to keep the children quiet," Edward said as he shut the back door.

The three mothers heard Edward talking to Ethel and Aurek and cannot help letting their emotions escape. Their faces were flush and tears were like rain running down their cheeks. One could hear them say, "Thank you God for your goodness!"

Edward pulled up to the guard who was standing there holding a big red sign with the word "HALT" printed on it in white.

"May I see your papers, Sir?" the guard asked.

"Yes. Here they are and the ambulance behind is with us," Edward explained.

"What ambulance, Sir?" The guard asked.

Edward looked in the rear view mirror and saw the ambulance parked on the side of the road. Ethel was standing beside the ambulance, holding one of the little children by the hand, while he relieved himself.

The guard motioned for Aurek to pull the vehicle up to where he was standing. Edward went through the roadblock, pulled the car over to the right side of the road, got out, went back to where Aurek was parked and asked, "What's up?"

Aurek said, "I couldn't pull up there. These ladies have lost it. They can't sit still and they won't keep their mouths shut, so I had Ethel take one of the little ones out to go to the bathroom to give them time to calm down."

The guard continued to shine his light into Aurek's face and wave at him to pull up. Finally, the ladies quieted down and as Aurek pulled up he told the guard, "Sorry, nature called for the little guy."

Edward returned to the car and waited with Sylvia. The guard shined his light into the face of each woman and child asking Aurek, "Are they for the medical evaluation conference in Stuttgart?"

"Yes, they are," Aurek answered.

"May I see your papers?" the guard asked.

"The Captain has them," Aurek replied.

"You are the driver of this vehicle. You must keep a set of orders within the vehicle. What would happen if you and your Captain should be separated?" the guard asked.

"What should we do? We have no way of making copies out here," Aurek said.

"Go up the road about twenty kilometers and you will see a sign marked 238th Staff/SS Security Regiment. Follow the signs up to the Headquarters building. You can have copies typed for you there," the guard said, as he walked over to the car where Edward and Sylvia were waiting.

He told Edward what he had told Aurek and gave him the same directions.

As they left the Headquarters building Edward motioned for Aurek to follow him. Aurek had to tell the ladies to stop their singing and to be very quiet if this plan was going to work. He couldn't blame them; these ladies had just been pardoned along with their children. They knew their children would now have a life and they knew their husbands would follow soon.

A couple of nights later, when Ethel and Aurek were in their rooms and Sylvia and Edward were in the examination room, Edward got up and turned off the lights. He took Sylvia's hand, pulled her to her feet, and led her down the hall. As he opened the door to his room, he said, "I think it will be safe if you come in."

She looked at him and said, "What about Ethel and Aurek?"

He knew they were asleep by now, so he put his arms around her and kissed her. He let go for a moment and reached over her shoulder to close the door.

The next morning Edward and Sylvia were up and showered long before Ethel and Aurek. In fact, they were on their way back from the mess hall when they saw Aurek and Ethel leaving the medical facility.

Lukas stood on the porch of his office and yelled, "Lieutenant Borg wait up and I'll join you two."

Edward said to Sylvia, "Let's go back to the mess hall and have coffee. I want to find what Lukas is up to."

Edward and Sylvia found a table with enough room for everyone. Ethel was the first of the three to arrive. Lukas rushed over so he would be able to sit next to Ethel. Aurek sat at the end of the table and asked Lukas what he wanted?

Lukas said, "Oh nothing. I just thought I would join you both for breakfast." Lukas' true thought was of how nice it would be if it was only Ethel and him and asked her, "Would you care to join me when I go into town today?"

Edward spoke up and said, "I don't believe Lieutenant Bamberger's husband would approve of that Hauptsturmfurhrer Wiesbaden!"

"Speaking of your husband Lieutenant, what unit is he in?" Lukas asked.

"He is not in the military," Ethel replied.

"Is there something wrong with him?" Lukas asked.

"He is an amputee, both legs!" she answered.

"I see," said Lukas and added, "I am sorry. Maybe we could all go to town someday. There's nothing wrong with that, is there Captain Von Mueller?" Lukas asked, as he got up and left, not waiting for an answer from Edward.

"He is not going to give up on you," Edward said, as he finished off his cup of coffee.

Edward picked out the three husbands and a mother with two children at roll call formation. Outside the medical facility the men asked where their wives and children had been taken.

"They are all right and you will be joining them soon. They are in Stuttgart," Edward said.

"Why were they taken to Stuttgart?" one of the men asked.

Edward said, "We will discuss this once we are inside."

The man asking the questions said, "No. I want to know where my wife and son are now and why you have shipped them off to Stuttgart?"

The man became very loud and got the attention of some of the guards standing their post nearby. Edward tried to calm him down, but before he could say anything, one of the guards hit the man in the back of the head with the butt of his rifle, knocking him to the ground. The guard held his rifle with his left hand, took his right hand and pulled the bolt action rod back, pushed it forward chambering a round, and was just about to pull the trigger when Edward yelled, "Stop! Return to your post."

He motioned for Aurek to help the prisoner to his feet and told him to move him inside the medical facility. Ethel saw what was going on with the prisoner from the porch. She went back inside and prepared an injection for him. It seemed to take less than a minute for it to take effect. Edward ordered the others to shower as he helped Aurek take the prisoner to a room.

"Let him sleep it off, but I want him to be constrained just in case he wishes to continue his quest when he wakes up," said Edward.

While the prisoners were in the shower, Edward talked to the others about the incident saying, "Well, that was a first. I am sure Captain Malzmueller will hear about it from the guard, but I had no other choice. I couldn't let him shoot him. If the other prisoners had heard that shot we would never get any of them to answer to their names in the future. I am sure that would be great for Captain Malzmueller. He would just give us the sickest and the weakest, but we don't have the luxury or the time to convalesce the prisoners for traveling across the border into Switzerland."

"What are you going to tell Malzmueller if he questions you?"

Sylvia asked. Before Edward could answer, the prisoners came out of the dressing area carrying all their old cloths in their arms.

Edward said, "Drop all your old things into the drum setting in the corner of the dressing room."

Sylvia, Ethel, and Aurek started the process of checking them in. You could see by the expression on their face they were confused and couldn't really understand what just happened to the other prisoner. They probably wanted to ask question, but were afraid that the same could happen to them.

Edward went into the room where they had placed Mr. Wiesenthal to check him over when he noticed he was not breathing and he couldn't find a pulse. He yelled for Ethel to come into the room.

Ethel checked him out and said, "He has expired. The blow to the head must have caused a cerebral aneurysm."

Edward felt sick and had to sit down. He placed his arm on the edge of the bed and rested his head on his forearm. He said, "Why, oh why, did he have to cause such a commotion? Why didn't I just tell him everything was going to be all right and that his wife and son were in Switzerland?"

Ethel said, as she pulled the sheet up over Mr. Wiesenthal face, "It's not your fault Edward. There was nothing any of us could have said or done to make matters any different."

Edward could hear someone banging on the front door of the medical facility. Aurek opened the door to see Captain Malzmueller standing there, asking to see Captain Von Mueller.

"Coming," said Edward, as he walked out onto the porch and closed the door behind him.

"I received a report from one of my guards that you had a prisoner who got out of control today," Malzmueller said, as he stepped down off the porch and lit a cigarette.

"I wouldn't say he was out of control. I believe your guard overreacted to a situation I felt I had in hand. You may inform your guard he was the cause of the patient's death. The next time he interferes with one of my patients I'll press charges and see if maybe he would like serving on the eastern front," replied Edward.

"It's still my understanding, you lost control of a patient or prisoner or what ever you call them and the guard came to your aid," said Malzmueller.

"I'll ask you this. Did he say he heard me call out to him for assistance? I think not. You may also inform him that he has destroyed the past six months or more of medical research that was performed on this particular patient's son. Now because I don't have the father, I have nothing!"

Malzmueller tapped out his cigarette on the edge of the porch, looked Edward in the eye, and said, "Now you listen to me. I don't care one bit about how much research you have lost or for that matter how many patients you lose. If you ever give one of my guards a command again, we will see who may want to go to the eastern front." Malzmueller turned and walked away before Edward had a chance to reply.

Edward thought about it for a minute and decided he wouldn't pursue the matter mater any farther. It could be dangerous for all of them if he brought too much attention to the situation.

Edward walked over to Lukas's office, not mentioning his discussion with Malzmueller, and requested he have a couple of men pick up the body of Mr. Wiesenthal.

Lukas does not ask Edward any questions about how the prisoner died. He simply picked up the phone, called down to the quarry, and ordered them to send two prisoners to the medical facility to pick up a body and deliver it to the crematoria.

Edward wasn't sure how much more he and the others could take before blowing their assignment. They had to get away from the camp for a period of time. He thought he would check with

Julius to see if they could work out something. He mentioned it to the others and asked how they would like to take a leave from all this? They all agreed.

Sylvia asked, "Do you think we could all go at once?"

Edward said, "That is what I am going to ask Julius tonight."

Julius thought it was a good idea and it would be best for them all to go at one time. He knew Lukas wasn't going to say anything and added they could use the house in Obereberfing.

Edward told the others they were all going to Obereberfing for a month. Then Edward met with Lukas and told him they would be suspending all testing for one month while and he and his staff took a thirty day leave. He informed Lukas they would make the next medical evaluation and would depart to go on their leave from there. Edward asked Lukas to have his clerk type up leave papers and asked Lukas to sign them. It was obvious Lukas felt good he was signing leave papers for Edward and his staff.

Edward picked out one additional prisoner to replace Mr. Wiesenthal.

Sylvia and the others started processing them through the medical facility that afternoon. They were issued clean clothes and ordered to shower. Edward told the others, while the patients were taking showers, to let them take their time eating dinner tonight and afterwards they could sit and talk before going to bed. By the time they had completed their showers their dinner had been delivered. Even though there were windows in the examining room they had been painted over so no one could see in. Edward thought it would be nice to witness the patients enjoying themselves for a change.

After a couple of days, the patients were given their shots and were out of it for the next week or so. The shots were wearing off just as the patients were delivered to Julius' people, who would prepare all the necessary paper work that would allow them to cross the border into Switzerland.

9

As they drove up the driveway to the Obereberfing house, Edward could see Julius standing on the porch. He stopped the car and let Sylvia out. Aurek did the same with the ambulance, let Ethel out, and followed Edward behind the house to park the vehicles in the detached garage.

Julius greeted the girls and gave them both a big hug saying, "You all have done so well with this assignment and that goes for you two, also," as he pointed at Edward and Aurek when he saw them approaching. They shook hands and also received a big hug.

Julius said, "Come in. Come inside where we can talk. I want to hear about everything." Once they were inside, Julius told them to go to their rooms and return to the study for drinks.

Julius waited until everyone was in the study to introduce the new housekeeper. "This is Hilga, everyone, and these are her two nieces, Chaviva and Adira. They will be preparing all your meals and taking care of your needs for the next thirty days. Enjoy," said Julius. "Let's have a drink before dinner. Tell me Edward, how was it with Lukas when you told him about taking off for thirty days."

Edward said, "I was surprised. He didn't seem to mind we were going to be gone for thirty days. But let me tell you, we had to get out of there Julius."

Julius nodded in agreement and said, "I know how hard it must be for you all. I must tell you, you are doing something that must take every fiber in your being to endure and we are so thankful to each one of you. You must know how much the families you have helped appreciate you being there."

Julius wanted to know how the payroll system he had set up for them was working. Edward said, "It couldn't be any better. Having our pay distributed by Lukas each month is a work of art. I asked him to sign our leave papers and you would have thought Hitler himself had asked him to sign them. His face was beaming."

Edward and the others continued to speak German while they were on their thirty day leave, otherwise when they returned it would be very easy to slip up and blow the whole operation. It helped that Hilga and her nieces also spoke German.

Upon their return, the guard at the front gate told Edward the commandant wanted to see him as soon as he returned. Edward said to the guard, "Thank you. I'll go there straight away."

He turned to Sylvia and said, "I'll drop you at the medical facility so you can tell Aurek and Ethel what's going on," as he got out of the car and walked over to Lukas' office.

Lukas was just walking out of his office when he saw Edward coming in the front door. "Come in. Come in Captain Von Mueller," Lukas said, as he stepped aside and motioned Edward into his office. Lukas walked back in and closed the door asking, "How was your leave?"

"Fine. Thank you," Edward said and asked, "What's up? The guard said you needed to see me right away."

"Yes, I do. We had an incident the day before yesterday. Captain Malzmueller found one of his guards dead. The cause of death has not been determined as of yet and Doctor Hanh asked me to have you or one of your staff assist him in the autopsy," replied Lukas.

Edward was grateful it could be one of his staff and told Lukas he would talk to Hanh right away and have Lieutenant Bamberger assist him.

Lukas said, "That will be great. I'll call him and tell him you will be right over."

Edward told the others what Lukas wanted and asked Ethel, "Can you handle assisting Doctor Hanh with an autopsy?"

She replied, "I don't have any training in pathology, but there should be no problem. I will go with you to talk to the doctor and get the details." Doctor Hanh didn't seem to be in good health himself and was muddled about things. Ethel explained she did not have any pathology training but she would assist him if he explained exactly what she was to do.

Hanh stood there looking at her and finally asked, "When would you be available?"

Edward spoke up and said, "Anytime you want to get started doctor."

"Good then. Let's do it first thing in the morning and don't worry about any pathology training. I have enough for the both of us. I just need someone to take notes and that understands medical terms," said Hahn. The doctor didn't seem to be sure about things one minute and then the next he appeared to be in full control of all his faculties.

The next afternoon, Hanh determined the guard suffered inflammation of the liver caused by infectious or toxic agents, characterized by jaundice and liver enlargement, and better know as Hepatitis. Hanh told Lukas, "Most likely he was exposed to the gases they are administering. Maybe you should instruct Captain Malzmueller to rotate his guards more often. Also, tell Captain Von Mueller he is very fortunate to have someone like Lieutenant Bamberger on his staff."

No more than a week had passed after their return when Edward and the others noticed all the prisoners were lined up in the roll call area. It appeared they were receiving shots, but as Edward got closer to the tables he could see the prisoners were being identified with a number that was tattooed on the inside of their forearm.

Edward asked one of the guards, "What is going on?"

"Direction from Berlin. We are to identify each prisoner with a pre- assigned number. Auschwitz and Dachau were the first to use this system of identifying the Jewish prisoners," said the guard.

Edward turned to Aurek and said, "Get a car ready. We have to go to town right away."

Sylvia asked, "Are we all going?"

"No. I'll go alone. I have to let Julius know what is going on." Edward didn't wait until after dark like he normally would. He knew this was important news and had to talk to Julius right away.

Julius listened and when Edward finished said, "We knew about Dachau and Auschwitz but didn't think they would do the same at Mauthausen because they have such a mix of nationalities. I can see the other camps doing this as the prisoners are ninety-five percent Jewish but Mauthausen is thirty percent at the most. We will continue as we have taking them out of Mauthausen, but with these identifying numbers we will have to change our method of getting them out of the country." Edward and the others continued to deliver the prisoners to the same location just outside Stuttgart and were never informed what changes were made on getting them out of the country.

Lukas sent a message to Edward informing him there would be entertainment for the troops next Saturday night at the dining hall and he hoped that Edward and his staff could attend. He explained dinner would be served at 5:00 PM in order to prepare the dining hall for the show. Edward accepted Lukas' invitation and thought it would be good for him and the others to get this place off their minds for a while.

On the night of the event, Edward and the others walked back to the dining hall after dinner early enough to get good seats up front. As the curtain opened Edward groaned loud enough for Aurek to hear where he was sitting three seats to Edward's right.

Sylvia asked, "What is wrong?"

Edward did not answer her but took the program he held and placed it over the lower portion of his face. Thank God the spotlight was in the eyes of the Master of Ceremony so he could not see Edward sitting in the audience. Edward waited until the first act was introduced and watched the MC walk behind the curtain before he got up and excused himself. He told the others to stay and he would be at the medical facility. He added that he wasn't feeling well, just in case others heard and wondered why he left so abruptly.

After the show, Sylvia knocked on Edward's door and asked, "Are you in there?" Edward opened the door and saw Sylvia and the others standing in the hall.

"What happened? Why did you get up and leave like that?" Sylvia asked.

"I am sorry, but the MC knows me. We worked together in a number of shows. I thought I was going to pass out. I had to get out of there quickly. Are they still at the dinning hall?" said Edward.

Aurek spoke up and said, "Yes. They are serving refreshments.

We didn't take the time to partake because we wanted to know what happened to you?"

"Do you think he saw you?" Sylvia asked.

"No. I am sure the spotlight was too bright for him to see much of anything in the audience, but I wasn't going to sit there and wait until he worked the audience. That was his specialty," replied Edward.

"You are right there. He had Lukas so confused he didn't know what to say," Aurek said and asked, "Does anyone want a cup of coffee?"

Edward said, "I think I want something a little stronger than coffee." He looked at Sylvia and asked, "Do you care to join me?"

"Yes, I think I will. How about you Ethel?" Sylvia asked.

Ethel replied, "Yes, I think I will join you. If you don't mind?"

"Of course not," Edward said and added, "Aurek, are you sure you want to bother with coffee?"

Aurek said, "Okay. I'm game. Let's go have some drinks."

"Good. It's early enough. Why don't we all go downtown and get away from this place for a while?" said Edward.

"I'll get a car," Aurek said, as he walked toward the front door.

After they drove out the main gate, Edward told Aurek, "Let's go to the Gasthofzur Hotel."

Edward and the others were just settling in with their first round of drinks when they heard loud voices coming from the main lobby of the hotel. They could see the lobby from where they sat and it was Lukas and some of his staff along with the entertainers from the show. Edward didn't wait for them to enter the bar.

He stood up and said to the others, "I'll be in the car. Take your time and enjoy your drinks," as he walked out the back door into the alley.

The group entered the bar area and started pulling tables

together when Lukas looked over and saw Aurek and the girls. He walked in their direction and said, "Well, well. This is a pleasant surprise. Why don't you join us for drinks?"

Sylvia spoke up and said, "We were just finishing up, but thank you for the offer."

"Aha. Come on over and meet the group," replied Lukas.

"Okay. If you insist," she said, as he saw that their glasses were full. She looked at Aurek and Ethel and said, "Shall we?"

Lukas made sure that Ethel had a seat next to him. While the other two got seated, he introduced everyone as a group, "This is part of our medical staff and these are the entertainers." He asked, "Where is Captain Von Mueller?"

Sylvia spoke up and said, "He is not feeling well, so he stayed at camp."

Captain Malzmueller said, "Yes. I saw him leave the show early and I wondered what was wrong."

Sylvia assured them Edward would be all right. Aurek and the girls finished their drinks and did not order more. Sylvia stood up, announced they would be leaving, and told the entertainers how much she and the others had enjoyed their show.

"Are you sure I can't talk you into staying for just one more drink?" Lukas asked.

"No, thank you, We must be getting back now," Sylvia said and turned to walk, as Aurek and Ethel followed.

Edward wasn't sitting in the car but on a bench in a dark area of the parking lot, just in case Lukas insisted on seeing the girls to the car. He waited a few seconds and saw they were alone before joining them at the car.

"Well, this has certainly been an interesting night," Edward said, as he flopped down on the back seat. "If it is all the same to you, Ethel, I'll ride back here and you can sit up front with Aurek."

Sylvia told Edward, "We saw the MC of the show, but he was

too interested in a young lady from the show to pay any attention to us."

"I did hear him say they would be performing for the troops in Frankfort tomorrow night, so you won't have to worry about him being around," Ethel said, as she shut the door of the car.

More than two years had passed. Lukas was transferred to Treblinka extermination camp. George Bachmann moved up to SS-Hauptsturmfuehrer and a new Deputy was appointed. The new deputy was none other than Captain Malzmueller. Edward was promoted to Major and Aurek and the girls to Captain. There hadn't been any problems between Edward and Malzmueller for a year or so. Now that Edward outranked him, there wouldn't be any problems because Malzmueller respected higher-ranking officers.

A train load of new prisoners arrived at the camp. Edward and the others saw evidence of the German imposed restrictions on the Jews in the identifying Jewish star they were ordered to wear on their clothing. This particular day was the most solemn holiday of Jewish religion, the Day of Atonement. The Germans began to round up the families in the ghettos throughout Germany and those who resisted or tried to hide, were shot.

Edward and his group were making final preparations for their trip, as they were departing early in the morning with another six prisoners. Deputy Malzmueller entered the medical facility and announced, "I have a bit of good news. Former Hauptsturmfuehrer Lukas Zieres called and said he would be attending the medical evaluation conference in Stuttgart tomorrow. He has invited me to attend as his guest."

Edward said, "That is good news. What time will you be leaving?"

"The same time as you. We might as well share the same car up, but most likely I'll take the train back since I would like to spend some time with Lukas," Malzmueller said, as he turned and walked out the door whistling.

Aurek did not wait for Edward to tell him to get a car. He said, "I'll get the car!" as he rushed out door.

Edward told Julius the bad news. "Do you know where Lukas is staying?" Julius asked.

"No. I don't," Edward answered.

"It is all right. We can find that out in time. You will go through a roadblock tomorrow morning and we will take care of Malzmueller there," said Julius.

"How will I know it is our roadblock?" Edward asked.

"Louis will be there," Julius said.

Edward said, "I better get back to camp. I am sure Malzmueller will want to talk about the trip."

Edward was correct in his assumption. When he got back to camp Malzmueller had been in the medical facilities asking for Edward and told Sylvia have him come over to his office as soon as he got back. Edward told them what Julius said about the roadblock and left to go to the Deputy's office.

"Come in. Come in," Malzmueller said, as he pulled open his desk drawer and reached in to bring out a bottle of wine with two glasses, acting as if no animosity had ever happened between him and Edward. "Tell me, Major. Am I going to get sick watching these demonstrations?"

Edward replied, "You may. But they are called evaluations."

"Evaluation, demonstrations. What is the difference?" said Malzmueller.

"Well, I would say there are not going to be any operations performed for your pleasure. The doctors assigned to the Stuttgart conference evaluate each camp's tests and the experiments performed on the prisoner. In fact, you may find it very boring," answered Edward.

"Well. We'll see about that. What do you do at the conference?" asked Malzmueller.

"I explain to the staff what drugs I have given the prisoners and what affect the drugs have on them," Edward said, as he poured another glass of wine. He wished he had something stronger since he had to put up with the likes of Malzmueller.

"How can the doctors evaluate the prisoners if they did not see how they acted prior to you administering drugs to them?" asked Malzmueller.

"Not all tests are for brain deterioration. I'll admit these are harder to evaluate because they are unlike the tests using nerve and mustard gases, where the results are quite prevalent. Also, they do accept my initial evaluation of the prisoners," said Edward. "Well, I better turn in now. We will leave quite early tomorrow morning. Good night," remarked Edward, as he held his glass up, finished it off with one swallow, And turned to walk out.

10

The rain beat against the windshield so hard Edward could hardly see the road and Aurek following behind in the ambulance wasn't doing any better. Edward saw the roadblock, but wasn't sure if it was the one Julius had set up. The closer he got, the more nervous he felt. Finally, he saw Louis and wondered what was going to happen now. Louis motioned for the car to pull over to the side of the road. Louis walked over to the passenger side of the car and ordered Malzmueller to roll down the window and asked, "Are you Captain Malzmueller?"

"Yes, I am. What is the problem?" he asked.

"Nothing, Sir. Do you mind stepping out of the car for a moment?" Malzmueller was not out of the car for one second when Edward heard a zap sound. Louis had placed a pistol with a silencer on it to the back of Malzmueller head and with one shot blew his forehead wide open. Neither Edward, nor Sylvia could see anything, but Aurek and Ethel saw it all. Aurek thought he was going to be ill. Louis and another man took his body and put it in the back of a military truck. Lewis walked over to Edward's car to get Malzmueller's bags. Edward handed him one small overnight bag and one hang up bag.

Louis said, "Thank you," as he motioned for Edward and Aurek to leave.

Aurek was so upset that both his legs started jumping and he could hardly control his speed, let alone steer the vehicle. He had a flashback to his hometown of Szezecin, Poland. He had witnessed his father's death, in the same manner as Malzmueller's, while he was home from Berlin where he attended school. He and his mother and younger brother looked out between the boards of the false wall their father had made in his workshop, so they could hide when the Germans came. They could see anyone coming up the road and Aurek's father knew he would have time to hide them before the Germans reached the house.

Aurek's mother was a lady in her late forties with long brown hair she wore in pigtails. His younger brother Erek, a boy of fourteen, was slender unlike Aurek who had a stocky build. They saw the soldiers go into the house and come out in a few minutes with Aurek's father. The soldiers pushed him to the ground in front of a German SS officer. They could not hear what he said, but saw him take his pistol out, place it to the back of their father's head, and pull the trigger. His mother gasped for air and almost passed out. Aurek's had to place his hand over his younger brother's mouth to muffle his sobbing. The Germans took what they wanted, including the livestock and left.

Aurek's mother whispered, "We will wait until after dark to make sure no one can see us before we try to get out."

Aurek helped his mother carry his father's body into the house, where they wrapped him in sheets and left him on the bed. There was no time for a burial. They had to leave right away.

Aurek's mother said, "We will have to travel tonight. We have to get to Uncle Liuz's house. He will help us."

They rode their bikes and traveled on all the back roads. They had problems seeing since they had cried so much their eyes were swollen. It took them a little more than an hour to get there. Like Aurek's family, his uncle's family lived on a farm.

Aurek's mother pushed her bike into the woods along side the road to the house and said, "Follow me. We can hide our bikes here. I don't see any German vehicles, so it is safe to approach the house."

She knocked on the back door and yelled, "Liuz. Liuz. This is Luisa, open the door." The back door opened and Luisa saw her sister-in-law, Bogna. Luisa started to cry and asked, "Where is Liuz?"

Before she answered, her sister-in-law, Bogna, held the door open and said to Luisa and the boys, "Get in quickly." Once they were inside, she closed and latched the door.

Bogna could see by Luisa and the boys' faces something had happened. She asked, "What is it? What has happened?"

"Oh Bogna," said Aurek's mother, although she could not finish speaking and started to fall. Bogna grabbed her and with Aurek's help, put her down on the couch.

Aurek's spoke up and said, "Father is dead. The Germans did it. He hid us in his workshop before they arrived and we could see everything."

Bogna reached out, put her arms around Aurek and his younger brother, and told them how sorry she was for their loss. Luisa sat up on the couch, held her hands to her face, and said, "It was awful. We had to leave him at the house. Where is Liuz?"

Bogna sat down next to Luisa and told her Liuz was at a meeting of the resistance movement and should be home any minute.

"Aurek. You and Erek go and get our things we left by the bikes," his mother said, as she wiped her face with the wash cloth Bogna handed her.

Aurek and Erek went out the back door and headed toward where they left the bikes. After the boys left, Luisa said to Bogna, "It was awful and hard for the boys to witness the death of their father. What are we going to do?"

Bogna said, "Liuz will think of something. The resistance movement will help."

Liuz came down the road on his bike and saw the boys walking toward the house. He wasn't sure at first if it was them, but recognized Aurek. Aurek ran over to his Uncle and told him what happened. Their uncle stepped off the bike, letting it fall to the ground, as he held Aurek and Erek in his arms and said, "Hurry. Let's get into the house."

Once they were inside he saw his sister sitting on the couch and he rushed over and held her in his arms. Liuz said, "Aurek told me what happened. We can get help from my friends, but we will have to move fast. I know it will be hard, but try to get some rest. Aurek will go with me to the Krakowski farm. Most of the men will still be there."

Liuz said to Aurek, "Come on. We have to get help from my friends," as he hugged and kissed Bogna and reached down to give Luisa a hug.

Aurek stood quietly next to the big overstuffed chair his uncle was sitting in, listening to him explain what had happened and asking what they could do to help get his sister and her youngest boy out of the country? He quickly added, "Aurek will be staying here. We can use him in the movement since he speaks German very well."

An older man with white hair and beard spoke up and said, "I'll contact Julius in the morning he will have an idea of what to do. Go back home and wait until you hear from me."

First thing the next morning, Liuz looked out the window and saw Mr. Krakowski's grain truck coming down the drive toward his farm. He went down to meet him. Mr. Krakowski got out of the truck and said, "I spoke to Julius and he said to take your sister and her boys to Obereberfing in my grain truck."

Liuz asked him, "Did he say both boys?"

"Yes. Julius said he could use Aurek in his operation," said Mr. Krakowski.

Mr. Kraowski motioned for Liuz to lift the tailgate from the truck. Once it was removed he saw what looked like a high, deep, and wide box with a door located on the end. The box was high enough that a person could sit up right with plenty of headroom.

Krakowski said, "Once they are inside the box, we will replace the tailgate, cover the box with grain, and put the canvas cover back on."

"How are they going to breathe? Liuz asked.

"There are tubes connected to the bottom of the bed and they will receive plenty of fresh air. They will have food and water for the trip, also. Normally, it would take around seven hours but we can't take the chance of using the major highways, so it will most likely take us twice the normal time," Mr. Krakowski replied.

"What if they have to use the bathroom? Liuz asked.

"There is a bucket with a privacy curtain on one end of the box. I am sorry but that's all we have and I'll tell them when it will be safe to empty it. There is a drain spout in the corner of the box," answered Mr. Krakowski.

Before they got into the box, Luiz assured his sister he and the others would take care of her husband's body. Liuz asked Aurek, "Are you up to fighting with the resistance movement?"

Aurek said, "Yes. I will do anything." That was how he met Julius. Julius was able to get Aurek's mother and younger brother out of the country. Liuz and Bogna stayed on in Poland to fight with the movement.

Just up the road a bit, Aurek was brought back to the present situation when Ethel spoke up, told him to flash the headlights off and on, and pull over to the side of the road. Edward saw the lights in the mirror and pulled over to the side of the road. Ethel walked up to Edward's side of the car. She pulled her raincoat up over her shoulders, covered her head, looked inside the car, and said, "Aurek is in no condition to drive and I can't drive at all. We are going to have to stop for awhile until he gets it under control."

Sylvia spoke up and said, "I can drive."

Edward said, "Good. Ethel, you stay with the prisoners and Sylvia, send Aurek up here with me."

"What happen back there?" Edward asked.

"They shot and killed Malzmueller. Didn't you see it?" Ethel asked.

"No! I thought I heard something but did not know what it was," remarked Edward.

"Well, Aurek and I saw it first hand and it wasn't pretty. Aurek told me that is exactly what the Germans did to his father," said Ethel.

After the patients were dropped off, Aurek asked Edward, "What about Lukas? Isn't he going to say something if Malzmueller, or for that matter, we don't show up at the conference tomorrow?"

"Julius did not say how he was going to take care of Lukas but he did ask me where he was staying. So I am assuming he will be taken care of. We will stay outside Stuttgart tonight and head back tomorrow, giving us time to have attended the conference," said Edward.

On their way back to camp, Aurek shuttered as they drove by the place where they had "taken care" of Malzmueller earlier the day before.

A couple of days passed when George Bachmann entered the

medical facility and asked Edward, "Where in Stuttgart did you drop off Malzumeller last Friday?"

Edward said quickly, "Lange Strasse and Schmale Strasse. Why do you ask?"

"About what time would that have been?" Bachmann asked, not answering Edward's question.

Edward thought quickly and said, "Around twelve noon," allowing for a couple of hours after he was shot.

"Did he say he was going to meet anyone there?" asked Bachmann.

Edward replied, "Not there, where I let him out. He did say he was meeting Lukas and would be going to the Conference the next day."

Bachmann asked, "Did you see Malzumeller or Lukas at the conference?"

Before Edward said anything, the Commandant's clerk ran up on the porch of the medical facility, remembering the building was off limits to everyone, stopped to tap on the door and said, "Hauptsturmfuehrer Bachmann are you in there?"

Bachmann opened the door and asked, "What is it?"

"Reichsfuehrer Schmidt is on the telephone, Sir!" said the clerk.

"Out of the way!" Bachmann yelled, as he bolted to his office.

Edward wished he could hear what they were talking about and decided to go over to find out if Bachmann was through questioning him about Malzmueller. Edward walked over to the Commandant's office, but decided it would be unnecessary to go in, as Bachmann's office window faced the porch and he could hear Bachmann's conversation from where he stood.

"Yes, Sir. No, sir," was about all Edward heard Bachmann saying, before adding, "Are you sure? No, Sir I am not, I am not questioning you, Sir! I never knew either of them to be that way.

Lukas was always chasing woman. No, neither of them were ever married, Sir. Yes, sir. I have talked to Major Von Mueller and he dropped Malzmueller off around noon Friday. He told me Malzmueller was going to meet with Lukas later. No, Sir. Those are not his exact words, but he did say Malzmueller was going to go to the conference with Lukas. Yes, Sir. I know and again I am not questioning you, but it is so hard to believe, Yes, Sir. I know it is true now, but. . . ."

Edward heard Bachmann hang up the receiver and then heard him say goodbye. Evidently, Schmidt had already hung up the receiver on the other end. Giving Bachmann enough time to walk into the outer office, Edward opened the door and walked in as if he had just gotten there. He saw Bachmann walking toward him and asked, "Did you have any more questions in regards to Malzmueller, Sir?"

"No, but come in to my office. You have to hear this," said Bachmann.

Edward followed him into his office. Bachmann sat down behind his desk and said to Edward, "Shut the door behind you." Edward watched Bachmann reach into the drawer and pull out a bottle with two glasses. He asked, "Do you want to have a drink with me?"

Edward said, "Yes. Thank you."

Bachmann poured the drinks before he said anything else. Finally, he sat back into his chair and said, "They have found Malzmueller and guess where they found him?" Before Edward had time answer, Bachmann poured himself another drink and said, "You had better have another, also."

Edward set the glass down for Bachmann to fill it and asked, "Where did they find him?"

Bachmann said, "You're not going to believe this but they found him in bed, with Lukas, at the Hotel Körschtal," as he started to laugh hysterically. "It must have been a love triangle because both of them had their brains blown out. You think that's something! I told Schmidt he had to be kidding and he jumped all over me, telling me not to question him on the facts. What would you have said?"

Edward told Bachmann, "I would have said the same. In fact, I was going to ask you if you were sure you got the story correct."

"Exactly! Who wouldn't?" Bachmann asked and poured them both another drink. He yelled out to the clerk, "Bring me and Major Von Mueller another bottle, Shultz. Can you imagine going to bed with Malzmueller?" Bachmann was laughing so hard Edward could hardly make out what he was saying.

Edward knew he had consumed too much to drink, too fast, and all on an empty stomach. He said to Bachmann, "I have to get out of here and get some food into my stomach. You should do the same."

Bachmann kept on laughing and said, "You should have heard Schmidt trying to tell me the details. Of course, I said what came naturally to me, 'You've got to be kidding.'" Schultz brought another bottle into the room, but Edward waved him back out of the Commandant's office and said, "Take that bottle with you."

Edward reached over, grabbed Bachmann by the arm, and pulled him up to his feet. Edward wasn't in much better shape than Bachmann, but he was controlling his laughter, He thought about it for a minute and knew there was no way he could get Bachmann out of there and up to the mess hall. The way he was feeling he could not manage to walk that far himself. Edward called for Shultz to order dinner in for him and the Commandant. Edward sat Bachmann back down at his desk and let him laugh it off.

11

Early the next morning, Edward was in his room telling the others what Bachmann told him about Malzmueller and Lukas. Aurek asked, "What about the phone call from Schmidt you told us about? Couldn't that bring some attention to this place? That is the last thing we want to happen."

Edward started to answer but looked out the window, saw Louis pulling up in front on the medical facility, and instead said, "Here are our supplies. Please send Louis back to my room so I can tell him about Schmidt's phone call."

Aurek went out, started to help unload the truck, and said to Louis, "Major Von Mueller would like to see you inside. Go ahead we can get this," nodding at the other man Louis brought with him.

Louis stepped inside the examining room where Sylvia stood. She said, "Go on back to his room. He is waiting for you."

Louis knocked and heard Edward say, "Come in." He opened the door and stepped inside.

"What's up?" Edward asked.

"Have you heard about Malzmueller and Lukas?" Louis asked.

"Yes. I am glad you came by today, because Bachmann got a call from SS-Reichsfuhrer Schmidt yesterday notifying him about them. Schmidt got all over Bachmann for doubting his word," replied Edward.

Louis started laughing and said, "That was Julius talking to Bachmann. He figured he would put a scare in him, so he would think twice about calling and discussing the matter with Schmidt or anyone else."

Edward said, "I knew the situation in the hotel room was set up by Julius but had no idea he would pretend to be Schmidt!"

Louis started to laugh again and said, "You don't know Julius do you? Oh yes, I almost forgot to tell you. Just for old time's sake, Julius saw to it that some of Lukas' and Malzmueller's personal items were planted at both Fritz's and Otto's quarters. Now they will stand trial for murder. Of course, they will have alibis and get off but he felt he just had to do it for Felmen."

As they walked out onto the porch, Edward signed the papers Louis handed him and said, "Goodbye," and whispered, "Tell Julius hello from us all."

It was in the winter of '43. The cold bit into Edward like a sharp knife as he stood on the platform out in the roll call area. Edward thought of how disgusting it was that he had warm clothes, boots, heavy overcoat, gloves, and he could hardly stand this bitter cold. When in front of him stood men, women, and little children with hardly enough clothes on to cover them. As he called out the names, he heard them answer with shivering voices and saw them each run up to in front of the platform. There, just in front of the platform, was a fifty-five gallon drum where one of the guards had made a fire to keep warm, while he and some others waited until Edward had completed calling off the list of names.

Once they were back inside, Edward said to Aurek, "Make sure they get warm clothes and a hot meal, after their shower."

He turned to Ethel and Sylvia and said, "I want these woman and children to enjoy the warmth and be comfortable before you administer any shots. I want them to sit here and tell stories to their children."

Sylvia knew how Edward was feeling because they were all feeling the same way. Just once in a while, it was nice to let the prisoners do something different. To be like a family having a mother with her son or her daughter. They sat in the examining room or their own private room and talked in the warmth, with a full stomach. Best of all, they got to see them enjoy themselves. Otherwise, they only saw them back to a normal state for about a half an hour, at the most, before they were dropped off. They all felt that was not enough time. Sylvia thought it was unfair, after they had spent so much time; years now, they saw just a few minutes of gratification.

A loud knock at the front door of the facility broke Sylvia's concentration. "Major Von Mueller!" came the voice. It sounded like Shultz, the commandant's clerk.

Edward opened the door and said, "Yes. What is it?"

"Reichsfuehrer Schmidt is in Haupturmfuehrer Bachmann's office and would like to meet you, Sir," answered Schultz.

"Tell him I'll be there straight away," Edward said, as he headed for his room and got his overcoat.

Aurek and the others heard what Shultz said and asked Edward, "What do you think that is all about?"

"I don't know. If something should happen, Aurek I want you to go get the car and be ready to move out. Don't worry about me. Get the girls out first. Then call Julius and he will help you three to safety," said Edward.

Edward passed Schmidt's staff car and saw the driver sitting in the front seat. Edward's thought is of the driver and what he might have seen. He hoped the driver did not see him coming out of the medical facility in case Aurek and the girls have to leave. He figured he was overreacting and went into the outer office where Shultz opened the commandant's door and announced, " Major Von Mueller, Sir."

Edward saw the back of Schmidt's head as he sat in a large chair in front of Bachmann's desk. "Come in. Come in," Bachmann said, as he stood up and went to the corner of his desk. "Reichsfuehirer Schmidt, this is Major Von Mueller, whom you asked about."

Edward walked into the office and was adjacent the big chair, as it turned and almost passed out when he saw Julius sitting there. Bachmann saw Edward's weakened condition and asked, "Are you all right man? Let me pour you a drink." Bachmann looked at Schmidt and said, "I don't believe he is used to meeting such high-ranking officers, Sir."

"That must be it," Julius said, with a half smile. "Major Von Mueller. I am here to enlist you and your staff's services at Tereziny/Thereseinstadt. I am not sure if you have heard of the Gas-vans or not."

Edward finished off the first drink, reached for the bottle, poured another drink, and said, "Yes. I have."

"Good, I know from your records and your input at the Stuttgart Medical Evaluation Conferences over the past number of years, that you have made quite a name for you and your staff. That is the reason I have already talked with Doctor Mengele and coordinated it with SS-Reichsfuehrer Heinrich Himmler. Therefore, you and your staff shall proceed to Tereziny/Thereseinstadt immediately. Your replacements will be here within the week," replied Julius.

Edward asked, "What about the six prisoners we are working on at present? They are not quite ready for the next conference."

"You will take them with you. You may drop them off on your

way. I understand there are facilities for holding them for up to thirty days, correct?" said Julius.

"Yes, Sir. You are correct," replied Edward.

Bachmann remembering the time he questioned Schmidt was glad he was interested in Von Mueller and not him.

Julius said, "I would like to take a look at your medical facility."

Bachmann jumped up and said, "Yes, Sir," and started to walk toward the door.

Julius stood and said, "That's not necessary, Bachmann. Von Mueller can show me, but thank you anyway."

Bachmann was ecstatic and poured himself another drink because the less he had to do with Schmidt the better.

Sylvia and the others couldn't believe their eyes. The three women and their children were ushered off to their rooms, but did not seem to mind as they did not want to be in the room with a German officer. As soon as they were out of sight, Sylvia and Ethel gave Julius a big hug and could not stop crying.

Edward asked Julius, "What's this about Tereziny/Thereseinstadt?"

"Oh, just some mumbo jumbo. We are getting you out as soon as possible," Julius answered, as everyone looked at each other.

Edward asked, "Why?"

"The war will hopefully be over soon and most of the concentration camp will be liberated by the American or Russian forces. We certainly do not want you here when that happens. I am sure you could explain yourselves but there could be some reprisal from the prisoners before you had time to do so. Therefore, you will be going to Switzerland along with your last six prisoners," said Julius.

"Can't we take their husbands, also?" Edward asked.

Julius thought for a moment and said, "Yes. Let's do it! I am sure Bachmann would not mind if I tell him it was my suggestion."

Edward figured he would call out the three husbands and a couple with one child when he called for an emergency roll call. Bachmann wanted to know what was going on. Julius explained he thought it would be a good idea if Major Von Mueller would take along the husbands of the three women and children. Also, he would take a couple and one children, so he could get rid of them all at one time.

Bachmann said, "That is a splendid idea," and hurried the roll call along.

Edward said to Bachmann, as he left the formation, "We will leave the medical facility equipment and supplies for our replacements."

Bachmann said, "Fine. I am headed for the mess hall. Do you mind telling Schmidt that I am having a staff meeting there in five minutes?"

"No. Not at all," Edward said.

Edward told Julius, "We can fit all the prisoners and their children in the ambulance with Aurek and Ethel."

Julius remarked, "There will be twelve prisoners in the ambulance; it's going to be tight."

Julius said to Edward, "I hate to do this, but maybe you better give the adults shots so they won't try to overtake Aurek. You will be going from here to the Danube River, just on the other side of Linz. Stay on highway B-3 and where the highway dead-ends that will be Rechte Donaustrasse. Make a left and go one mile and turn right onto Hafenstrasse. Follow Hafenstrasse down to the water's edge. There you will see the boat, The Gray Goose. The skipper's name is Graben. He will take you down to the end of the Danube at Messkirch where Ganit and his people will meet you and get you and the prisoners into Switzerland."

Julius turned and said before he got into his staff car, "Good luck to each one of you and thank you beyond words. See you on the other side."

After administering the shots and giving them time to take effect, the prisoners were situated in the ambulance. Ethel wondered where Aurek was and looked up to see him walking down the hill from the mess hall carrying a couple of large brown bags. He walked over to the car where Edward and Sylvia waited, handed Edward one of the bags, and said, "Here are some fresh sandwiches and coffee. I'll take this bag for Ethel, the kids, and me."

Edward said, "That's fine," and started the engine of the car. He slowly pulled up to the front gate and waited for Aurek to pull up behind him.

Edward heard the phone at the guardhouse ring and saw the guard pick up the receiver. He heard the guard say, "Yes, Sir. He is here," and motioned for Edward to come to the phone. "It's Hauptsturmfuehrer Bachmann, Sir," the guard said, as he handed Edward the phone.

"Yes, Commandant?" Edward asked.

"Has Schmidt left yet?" Bachmann asked Edward.

"Yes, Sir. He has," Edward replied.

"Very well. Are you about to leave as well?" Bachmann asked. Edward answered, "Yes, we are."

"Well, Von Mueller. I want to wish you and your people the best. I don't envy you on your new task, you know, the vans," said Bachmann.

"Yes, Sir. I know," replied Edward.

"Well, take it easy," Bachmann said and hung up the phone.

Edward hung up the receiver, walked back to the ambulance, bent over, looked into the cab, and asked, "Well, do you two feel like Camp Angels?"

He did not wait for their answer. He walked to the car, where

Sylvia waited, got in, looked into her eyes, and said, "I wish we could have done more!" as they drove out the main gate for the last time.

THE END

Epilogue

Edward, Sylvia and Ethel made it into Switzerland where they joined their families. Edward and Sylvia were married, have two children, and now live in Israel. They were asked to return to attend the first Mauthausen Camp Memorial in 1954. They were the honored guests at the memorial.

Ethel now lives in the United States and was unable to attend the Memorial, as she was diagnosed with cancer and could not travel.

Aurek did not go to Switzerland with the others. He stayed on to fight with the resistance movement. He was mistaken for a German soldier, along with Louis, and was shot and killed by the allied forces.

Mr. Krakowski, head of the Polish resistance, was captured and executed in the Town Square along with Aurek's Aunt Bogna and Uncle Liuz shortly before the end of the war.

Preben made it to Switzerland with Felmen. He currently lives in Bern with his wife and five children. He owns and operates a small coffeehouse.

Felmen lives in the United States. He is the CEO of a major Hollywood Studio. Felmen created the roll of SS-Reichsfurhrer

Schmidt for Julius while he was still in Switzerland. For many years, some of Germany's high-ranking officers, even Hitler himself, believed Schmidt was authentic and during their trials gave his name and blamed him for most of the deaths in the concentration camps.

Julius died of cancer in 1968. He was sixty-eight years old. He asked that a photo of him, as SS-Reichsfuehrer Schmidt, and Adolf Hitler be donated to the Holocaust Memorial Museum in Los Angeles, California.

The team who worked at Mauthausen Concentration Camp for three years and eleven months was instrumental in freeing 288 prisoners destined to be put to death in the gas chambers or starved to death at the camp.

All but 23 of the 288 prisoners released were able to attend the Memorial. When those attending saw Edward and Sylvia they started chanting, "CAMP ANGELS! CAMP ANGELS! CAMP ANGELS!"